Praise for Ben Tanzer's
The New York Stories

"With great humor and the natural voice of your closest confidant, Ben Tanzer brings us stories set in our shared fictional hometown of Two Rivers, NY. With tenderness and heart, Ben brings us real people and their poignant, messy struggles, reminding us of the folly of our youth and the beauty in even our most mundane histories. Though my family left when I was small for the big city, Tanzer has given this reader the gift of a sliding door here, and I think you'll feel the same way, wherever you're from." —Elizabeth Crane, author of *We Only Know So Much*

"Ben Tanzer's stories are both familiar and surprising, a scarf and a knife. Stories full of people we know, love. People we don't want to know, don't want to love. Stories full of desire and sadness and almost. Stories over beers and tequila, stories inside sex and storms. Ben! He is one of my favorites for all sorts of reasons and one of those reasons is yes and another is hell yes." —Leesa Cross-Smith, author of *Every Kiss A War*

"The millions of unseen things that happen inside the heart finally start to come clear in Ben Tanzer's *The New York Stories*. Everyone here—from the teenage girls to the grown men trying to sleep with them, from the guy in therapy to the therapist—is filled with a desire so painful it will make you ache. Come to Thirsty's and drink a Yuengling because it might be all there is. Ben Tanzer knows that what we love most is what destroys us and what makes us feel most alive. He's reached into our music collections and pulled out the soul and the funk and the loud guitars and set it to prose that pulls us all across the page. Be prepared to laugh and cry and be swept away." —Dave Newman, author of *The Factory Poems*

"In his beautiful and deeply American *The New York Stories*, Ben Tanzer returns to the upstate place where it all began: childhood, adolescence, the buds of adulthood. Caterpillar guts ooze out on the pavement, as do restless hearts. 'Thirsty's still serves beer, the Susquehanna River still flows, and you are here by the window, watching, waiting, wondering how you got here at all.' Characters may come and go and circle back in the fictional town of Two Rivers, but through it all Tanzer's voice is a transporting constant: intimate, immediate, full of wisdom and grace. Spanning three masterful volumes, brimming with lust and longing, humor and heartbreak and a healthy helping of what-ifs, this collection is for anyone who has lived and loved or loved and lost or any whirling, churning combination of the three. In other words, it's for all of us." —Sara Lippmann, author of *Doll Palace*

"Tanzer's growing to become one of my favourite non-genre writers working today. He's a domestic tragedian, an author who 'gets' the peculiar melancholia of getting older and kissing goodbye who you once enjoyed being. ...The quiet nimbleness of Ben Tanzer's writing is not something that translates well through a review, it's something you have to experience for yourself. Please do. You can thank me afterwards." —Benoît Lelièvre, *Dead End Follies*

"*The New York Stories* is a three volume set, each published as separate books across a span of nearly nine years and because of this, the book builds a wonderful grand arc, narrative hindsight in a way that allows the whole thing to function as a story greater than the sum of its parts. We see not only the long protracted march of Two Rivers and its inhabitants, but, because of the time between when the volumes were written, the development of Tanzer as a fierce and world-class writer. This development is a beautiful thing to watch." —*Atticus Review*

"Ben Tanzer's New York is not the New York of Ellis Island or of Times Square. It's not the New York of Warhol or Scorsese or Giuliani. It's not the New York you know or have ever known. It's the New York you *should* know, the Tanzeriian New York of twisted invention, hilarious compassion, and intricate irony. Ben Tanzer has impossibly written yet another version of the great city, one that's a welcome addition to the proud canon of this salty berg." —Michael Czyzniejewski, author of *I Will Love You For the Rest of My Life: Breakup Stories*

"Long before the floodwaters start to build in Ben Tanzer's *New York Stories*, we sense their looming presence—the characters themselves drift and swirl about this dying town, trapped in the eddies of past indiscretion, borne along by longings and regrets, snagged upon their betrayals and petty resentments. Yet while one might be tempted to write them off as premature ghosts, here they live on, and like Carver's, these characters call to us from across the barstool, the pool table, the couch, the car seat. And by the end, Tanzer has made a convincing case that a deluge of stories might be the very thing to save us." —Tim Horvath, author of *Understories*

Also by Ben Tanzer

*Published by CCLaP

THE NEW YORK STORIES

THREE VOLUMES IN ONE COLLECTION

BEN TANZER

CHICAGO CENTER FOR LITERATURE AND PHOTOGRAPHY
2015

Printed and distributed by the Chicago Center for
Literature and Photography. *First paperback edition, first
printing: June 2015.*

Cover: Laura Szumowski

ISBN: 978-1-939987-33-4

This collection is also available in a variety of electronic
formats, including EPUB for mobile devices, MOBI
for Kindles, and PDFs for both American and
European laserprinters. Find them all, plus a plethora of
supplemental information such as interviews, videos and
reviews, at:

cclapcenter.com/nystories

Contents

Publication History

"The Babysitter:" *THE2NDHAND*
"The Gift:" *THE2NDHAND*
"What We Thought We Knew:" *RAGAD*
"Change of Plans:" *Caketrain*
"Pac-Man Fever:" *The Truth Magazine*
"Life As He Had Known It:" *20dissidents*
"Shooting Stick:" *The Truth Magazine*
"So Different Now:" *Dogzplot*
"In a Single Bound:" *Necessary Fiction* (as "More Than Anything")
"Stevey:" *The Truth Magazine*
"Cool, Not Removed:" Artistically Declined Press
(as standalone ebook)
"Panties:" *The Truth Magazine*
"That's It:" *CellStories*
"Never Said:" *Girls With Insurance*
"Goddess:" *Annalemma*
"No Nothing:" *Another Chicago Magazine*
"Stabbed in the Back:" *Whiskey Paper*
"Freddie's Dead:" *Goreyesque*
"What We Talk About When We Talk About the Flood:"
The Heavy Contortionists
"We Were All Here:" *Used Furniture Review*
"Longing:" *Midwestern Gothic*
"Watching and Waiting:" *3Elements Review*
"Vision:" *Composite Arts Magazine*
"The Runner:" *The 27th Mile*
"Things Start:" *Heart*
"Untrammeled:" *Revenge of the Scammed*

Introduction

I IMAGINE that *The New York Stories* as a whole are no more about my hometown of Binghamton, NY than *The Warriors* is about New York City.

There are bars in common, diners, and the Susquehanna River, but *The New York Stories* are not literally about a place I haven't lived in twenty-five years, much less really don't know at all anymore.

However, it is my place of origin. It formed me and spit me out into the world.

It is where I survived elementary school and high school, and got into fights, where I learned to ride a bicycle and drive, started drinking and running and reading, had sex for the first time, poorly, fell in love, endlessly, experienced rejection, shattered femurs, amputated fingers, and broken hearts.

And that is all real, imprinted on my brain, and like the Seventies and Eighties, a filter for everything that came after it and is yet to come.

I see things through the eyes of the places I lingered in then, the Park Diner, Pudgie's, Thirsty's, Lupo's, Starnsie's, Sharkey's, Robby's Liquor Store, the Arena, the V Drive-in, I remember the girls I longed for, and the hopes and dreams that ping-ponged in my adolescent brain.

And so *The New York Stories* is all of that, memory, pain, lust, and violence, endlessly spewed out from my brain and mingled with my current obsessions, wants, confusions, hopes, and general fucked-upedness.

It is also ultimately an homage to Richard Linklater, and especially the *Before Sunrise, Before Sunset, Before Midnight* trilogy, and a look at how we grow and things change and warp, and the need to keep talking, and keep musing, as we try to make sense of all, or even any, of it.

It is also the outgrowth of my desire to create something where nothing existed before. And I'm not referring to the stories of small towns, or linked narratives, art about time and place, but something more selfish than all of that, my desire to create something that said something to me when I could barely get anything published at all.

Repetition Patterns was the culmination of that feeling and all of its Junot Diaz and Elizabeth Crane Brandt influenced sweaty desperation. Could I create something that hung together and was bigger than me? And could I find someone who might care about it as much as I did?

Talking about *Repetition Patterns*, reading an essay about an otherwise happy couple who decided to find out if they really were, and thinking about where the stories could go begat *So Different Now*, and the visceral jolt of Laura Szumowski's illustrations for the earlier iteration of *The New York Stories* combined with the release of *Before Midnight* and the flooding of Binghamton, especially the South Side where I grew up, begat *After the Flood*.

BEN TANZER

And here we are eight years and 50,000 plus words later, still longing, still desperate, still fighting, and releasing *The New York Stories* into the world, just as Binghamton once did me.

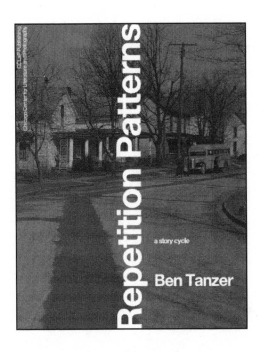

Repetition Patterns
2008

Repetition Patterns

I DO NOT LIKE P. FROM THE START—his neat little beard, his sweater vest, his loosened tie. His body language is too aggressive, too voluble and terribly off-putting. His facial expressions speak volumes more than he realizes, fluctuating between amusement and disdain at anything I say. He is too smug by half, all-knowing, and condescending. He sits there in judgment of me, a touch of anger always lurking on the periphery of his comments. And then there is his office, cold, uninviting, and minimalist; a couple of chairs, a desk, and miles of unused space.

I feel this way after the first session. I ignore it though. I don't trust my reaction. I don't trust myself. I am not good at doing so. I tell myself that it is the fear speaking, and that I am anxious about re-entering therapy. The thing is, I know this type, and I know what they are and are not capable of. I have always been drawn to people like P.

"You are a liar," P. says. He had asked me whether I thought my father had been a good man. I knew what he was expecting me to say. I even kind of knew what I wanted to say, but I stammered instead, and paused, and then said yes, yes, he was a good man. P. clearly does not agree. "He was not good to your mother," he says. And I can't disagree with him, not really.

"Tell me again why you're here," he says. "What did you call it—a tune-up?"

"Yes," I say. "With my dad having just died, and my wife and I talking about having our first child, I thought it was a good time to get back into therapy. You know." I pause. "A check-up, I guess."

"Right," P. says, shifting impatiently in his chair. "You realize, your dad and the baby, that's not why you are here."

"No?"

"No. You're here because you have always been in pain."

We are both silent. The afternoon light is slowly fading, and dusk is just beginning to cover the streets below. I start to cry. He is right. I know this and it hurts. He called me a liar, though, and that doesn't feel right, or good, and I am angry about it.

One week later I am back and sitting in his waiting room. NPR is on the radio and I am shivering. I am going to tell P. that his comment upset me. I am not looking forward to doing so. And then he appears. He's ready for me and I go in. We stare at each other. He gives me a look, his head thrust forward, his lips pursed, his face somewhat clenched. It's a shrug, really, and it's saying, You go first, what's on your mind. And so I go first.

"Why did you call me a liar?" No response. "I mean, is that necessary? It's very upsetting." He listens, he doesn't speak, he ponders, and then he says that he is sorry. Silence falls between us again. "I didn't like you from the start," I say. "There's an arrogance in you I find off-putting. I think I need to tell you that."

"I'm glad you did," P. says. "We can explore that in here." But we don't, not right then, not so much, and certainly not beyond some discussion about my ambivalence concerning being there in the first place.

I cannot tell P. that my wife Alice and I have decided to start trying to get pregnant. It is too scary, I am too intimidated, and I don't know how he will react or what he will say. And I don't really want to know. It is clear to me that I still have some concerns about having a baby, but I do not want him to point this out to me. I also don't want to know how he will go about pointing it out to me. So instead I tell him that I have decided to go on an eight-day backpacking trip through Italy. With everything that's been going on, I say, it's something I need to do. I'm leaving on Sunday.

The trip is escapist, P. tells me. "Your need to travel is a form of thrill-seeking behavior. You always talk about your desire to feel more excitement. This is how you hope to find it." He tells me to describe some of the people I consider happy, so I do. "Do you consider yourself happy?" he asks.

"I'm not sure," I say.

"Sure you are," he responds, in that false jovial manner of his that drives me crazy.

I'm really not sure. "Well, I don't know. Maybe I am. I could be depressed. I guess." I say this real low. He smiles and nods. I feel queasy. "I've never thought of myself as depressed," I say.

"Of course you haven't," P. says. "You're depressed." Another one of his condescending little smiles crosses his face.

Some months later Alice and I find out we are going to have a baby. I tell P. about it during a session. He is very happy for us, but says he is surprised to learn that we have been trying. "I didn't tell you we were going to start trying?" I say.

"No."

"I thought I did." As I sit there, I try and convince myself that I had, but it's no good. "Actually, I never really told you, I say, but remember when I said I was going to Italy? And that I needed to go? That's when we first decided to try."

"That's why you went?" he says.

"Yeah. Remember how you said it was thrill-seeking behavior and all that?"

"Sure," he says. "I wouldn't have said that, though, if I knew you were trying to get pregnant. That was a good reason to go."

I tell P. I am thinking that I might want to wind down my therapy as the year itself winds down, and that maybe we can work towards termination and closure. P. asks me if I think I am ready to move on. I say that I don't know, that I don't even know how I would know. I will always have some fear about leaving therapy, because leaving anything for me can be very difficult. "Of course, if I'm being totally honest," I say, "I've also learned that my insurance coverage is coming to an end, and that's causing me a lot of anxiety. I mean, what would your fee be if I just paid it out-of-pocket?"

"130 dollars an hour," he says.

I recoil. "That feels somewhat prohibitive to me," I say. "Is that negotiable?"

"How about we take a minute to discuss your expenses," he says. "For example, what do you pay in rent?" We run through a number of questions like this. "I did tell you what my rate was when you first came to me, didn't I?"

"No," I say. "You never told me."

"Really." He stares off into space for a moment. "Well, I always try to. Hmm. Tell me, then, what do you think is reasonable?"

I know most anything is going to feel prohibitive to me at this point, but I say a hundred dollars because I believe he will be offended by anything less.

"How about 115?" he says, smiling.

"105?" I reply.

"Let's say 110, then."

"Okay," I say, head spinning.

"Good. 110 it is. And I assume that you won't be taking any vacations from this point on, either."

"Pardon me?" I say.

"Vacations. If you feel you can afford one, then I'll expect you to pay my regular fee."

"Doesn't that..." I'm stunned. "Doesn't that seem extreme to you?"

"Of course not," he says, looking confused. "This is about your priorities. I'm willing to take less because you say it's a hardship for you, and so you have to be willing to give up things as well. Do you know what people are willing to give up to come and see me?"

I don't know, actually, nor does he answer the question. The session ends and I leave.

I walk in. I immediately get the smile. I tell P. that I would like to start by asking him a question.

"No," he replies. "We will start with me asking the first question."

"Why do we need to go in that order?" I ask.

"Because I am the therapist," P. says, "and the therapist asks the questions." I sigh and lean back in my chair, as he continues. "How did you feel when you left your session last week?"

"Upset," I say. "Angry. Confused. And how did you feel?" I

5

irritably add.

"Angry as well," he says, matter-of-factly.

"I thought so. That's why I wanted to ask the first question. Why were you so angry?"

"Because I felt you had manipulated me, he says. You wanted to negotiate my rate and I did and I felt angry about it."

"It feels daunting to me," I say. "I have anxieties about money and you know this."

"Let's talk about those anxieties for a moment, shall we?"

"No. No. I want to keep talking about this."

"Do you feel that everything is negotiable?"

"I guess. My experience has been that people are always willing to negotiate. That they even expect to. It's business, and since this is a business I was hoping you would feel the same way."

"And that's why I feel manipulated," P. says.

"And yet you engaged in a negotiation with me," I say. "You asked me what I felt I could pay and then you countered what I suggested."

"That's true," he says, adding nothing else.

"I expect my therapist to set his personal issues aside during a session," I say. "You didn't do that."

"Well, then I guess you don't think I'm a very good therapist."

"Well, I guess I...don't. And I don't plan to see you anymore."

There is a long pause, then he says, "I guess there isn't much else to say then."

"It's just..." I stare at the ceiling. "It was important to me that I tell you in person."

"Are you sure you want to leave therapy?" he says. "Are you ready for that?"

"I'm not leaving therapy," I say. "I just don't plan to continue with you."

He is silent for a moment. This conversation is the first time I have ever seen him taken aback. "You know," he says, "you're not the first patient to have a problem with my personal style. A number of people have had to work through issues like this with me. But if they're able to do that, they really can get a lot accomplished."

"That's okay," I say. "I really have decided to move on. I need to move on."

And then comes the most uncomfortable silence of the entire session; there is ten minutes left and nothing left to say. We sit there for a moment, and then another, and I think to myself that I ought to just stand up, just walk out the door and leave, but I'm not sure how to do so or what I should say. I feel anxious, and P. is staring at me, both of us just waiting for something to happen.

I fixate on the new chair he has bought himself, something I had noted a few sessions back. It's big and green. Plush. It looks terribly comfortable. I had told him that I had always wanted such a chair and we had laughed about it. "I'm going to leave," I say, and then in a bout of something, the need to break the tension, I guess, I try to make a joke. "I mean, I could stay and all, but since you have the more comfortable of the two chairs, maybe I'll just get going."

P. continues staring at me, still silent. His eyes narrow and fixate on me. He furrows his eyebrows. There is no smile. He says, "You really need to figure out why you have so much anger." And then he stands up and opens the door of his office. And I leave. And we are done.

A couple of months after I stop seeing P., I go to see J. He's wearing a tweed jacket, his hair is somewhat unruly, and his tie is tight around his neck. His office is small and cozy, one entire wall of shelves covered in books—Kafka, McCarthy, Roth. J. makes no jokes, he is not provocative, and I wonder if I can even work with such a person.

7

I feel good here, though. Safe.

"Where would you like to start?" J. says.

"I should probably start with my most recent experience in therapy," I say.

"Ok," J. says, "what do you want me to know?"

"P. was an asshole," I say, "and he was unnecessarily provocative, confusing his anger towards me with an actual approach to therapy."

"So, he didn't help you at all?" J. says.

I pause for a moment. Did P. help me? Did I need P. to be the way he was?

"I would rather talk about what a jerk he was," I say.

"Fine," J. says, "but first let me tell you about repetition patterns."

The Babysitter

TRACEY WAS OUR BABYSITTER. She was five years older than me, and I hated her. She had ratty dark red hair, way too many freckles, and no ass at all. Her mom had moved out when she was a kid, and her dad had been raising her ever since. She smoked cigarettes in the breezeway and invited her dumb friends over to tease my younger brother Timmy. There was Amy, with the boobs, and Liz, who always looked like she was on the verge of crying.

Timmy had a lisp—nothing too bad, and he was working on it—but Tracey would not give him a break, especially when Amy and Liz were over. "Okay, Timmy," Tracey would say. "Say 'Canada.' C'mon, cutie."

"Sure, Tracey," Timmy would reply. "Cananada. I mean Candada. I mean...I can't do it."

And Tracey would laugh and laugh.

9

Amy was the first girl in the neighborhood to get breasts, and she wasn't bad-looking either—she had olive-colored skin, this kinky sort of sun-bleached blonde corkscrew hair, and great dark eyebrows. But it was definitely her boobs that drew your attention. They were soft and round and large, like Nerf basketballs, and completely awesome. We all wanted to see them, of course, but no one wanted to see them more than my friend Billy. He talked about them all the time. "Hey, man," he'd say. "Did you see Amy today?"

"Yeah," I'd say. "Why?"

"Did you see what she was wearing?"

"Yeah. I think they call them t-shirts."

"Right, but that's a pretty tight t-shirt, isn't it? Did you see her boobs?"

"Yes, I did, and they're very nice, just like when you asked about them yesterday."

"Dude, I've got to see them. I'm dying here."

And to give Billy credit, he didn't just walk around the neighborhood talking to us about them—he talked to Amy about them too. "So," he'd say. "You going to let me see your boobs or what?"

"How many times do I have to say no?" Amy would say.

"A lot," Billy would say. "A lot."

And one day, Amy finally said, "Fine, let's get this over with," and took him back behind his house. They weren't gone long, but Billy didn't stop smiling for a week.

Billy's dad was named Larry. He was tall with wavy dark hair, handsome like a television doctor but a little more scrawny. Larry had played Triple-A ball for the Pirates, but then blew out his arm before he made it to the big show. That didn't matter to the other dads in the neighborhood, though. They loved him for getting so close, and they were happy to let Larry hold court in front of his house on Saturday afternoons, as he sucked down beer after beer and spewed forth his endless stream of crap.

"Reagan's a great man," Larry would say. "A leader. A real fucking leader. You can see it in his eyes, and you can see it in the way he talks to the camera. He's speaking to you, not at you. He gets you, you know? I'm not embarrassed to say I love that man." All the dads would nod in agreement, their golf shirts a bit too tight around the waists, their sunburned noses now peeling and turning ugly.

They didn't know, of course, that Larry had fucked half of their wives, and was now eyeing their daughters too. Billy knew, though. He would follow his dad around and watch him through the windows of the car. He didn't know how to feel about it.

Tracey's other friend Liz cried a lot, like I said, and she liked to wear black. She would cut herself, too, but she had to do something; she had a secret that she couldn't tell anyone about. And no, it wasn't how she had slept with Billy's dad Larry one time after babysitting for Billy's younger brother (though she had), or how she had slept with Tracey's boyfriend Frank too (though she had done that as well), one night following a party where Tracey had made fun of the (very slight) twitch in her eye she sometimes got when she was nervous.

No, it was something else entirely, something that was dark and wrong, and not to be repeated. Liz once had a baby sister named Tabitha, who she regularly watched because her parents were never around much at night. Liz didn't mind watching her, though, and in fact had developed a game for her and Tabitha to play before bedtime. Liz would hold a pillow over Tabitha's face and muffle her breathing for just a moment before pulling it off and yelling, "Peek-a-boo!" Tabitha would always cough for a moment as her little lungs gasped for air and then laugh hysterically. It was great fun.

Liz soon realized that if she held the pillow on Tabitha's face just a little longer each time, Tabitha would not only cough more, but laugh more as well. One night when Liz lifted the pillow, though, Tabitha didn't cough, or laugh, or do anything at all. Tabitha wasn't breathing and wouldn't start breathing no matter what Liz tried to do. She gave her mouth-to-mouth, she picked her up and walked around the room, she begged her to breathe. "C'mon, Tabitha," she whispered. "Quit fooling around. C'mon, baby, please breathe, please." But nothing worked.

After awhile Liz put Tabitha back into her crib, and crawled into bed not knowing what to do or who to call. She awoke the next morning to birds chirping and her mom screaming. When asked about the night before, Liz said she put Tabitha down as she always did (which was kind of true), had then gone to bed (which was also pretty much true), and hadn't heard a sound all night, which was definitely true. The coroner said it was probably SIDS; nothing else made sense. "Sometimes it just happens," he explained to a co-worker. "It's a tragedy, but sometimes there's simply no reason or sense to it at all."

One afternoon I am over at Billy's playing Pong, when Tracey, Amy, Liz, and Tracey's boyfriend Frank come by. Frank has long, stringy, dirty blonde hair and wire-framed glasses that turn to black when exposed to the light. He likes Pink Floyd. And he's lugging a case of cheap beer.

"What's up," Frank says to Billy when he answers the door. "We were hoping we could drink some beer here, man. What do you say?"

"Sure," Billy says, shrugging, as the four of them come in and make themselves comfortable on the living-room floor. Frank immediately slams a beer and then another. Tracey matches him beer for beer, and within ten minutes they're making out.

"Hey," she says to Billy. "Is there a room we can use?"

"I guess," Billy says. "My room is at the top of the stairs."

They leave and the rest of us sip our beers and stare at each other. No one has much to say.

Liz, the one who cries a lot, says, "Hey, you want to play spin the bottle?" to no one in particular. Amy, with the boobs, sighs and asks why the hell not. Liz spins an empty beer bottle and it points to Billy. They start to kiss. "Let's go upstairs," Liz says. And they do. Amy looks at me, shakes her head in disgust, and spins the bottle. It points off into space after finally coming to a halt.

"You can kiss me," she says. "But that's it. No touching, grabbing, pawing, or petting. Got it?"

"Yeah," I say, "I got it."

I've never kissed anyone before. I sometimes wondered if I ever would. I lean forward, mouth slightly open, and then Amy does too. Her lips are soft, like ripe melon. She lingers for a moment, and then her tongue lightly darts around the edges of my mouth. I lean in some more and run my hands along her lower back. She pulls away abruptly and looks at me as if she has just awoken from a light sleep.

"Jesus," she says. "I just made out with a little kid." She looks around, a little panicked. "This is our little secret, right?"

"Yeah," I say.

One day Tracey comes over to babysit with Amy and Liz in tow, and of course starts right in on Timmy. "Okay, baby," she says. "Can you say 'Spaghetti' for me?"

"Sure, Tracey. Saghetti. Saspetti. Spa..."

"Why don't you leave him alone?" Amy suddenly says, her voice shrill.

"Why don't you and your boobs shut up?" Tracey immediately replies, her eyes narrowing.

Everybody is silent and unmoving, unsure of what comes next. And then there's a scream. Oh, sick, Liz says, pointing. "A mouse just ran across the room." Tracey calls her boyfriend Frank and begs him to come over. He says sure and shows up a little while later, his BB gun with him and another case of beer. We sit awaiting the mouse's return. It does not return.

Somewhere along the way, as more and more beers get shotgunned, Amy starts touching Frank, but without Tracey noticing; subtly at first, a hand on the shoulder, a brief brush of his leg, and then more brazen, running her fingers through his hair and squeezing his inner thigh. There is eye contact, low breathy murmurs, and whispers; Tracey is still oblivious because of being half-trashed herself. Frank suddenly says he has to leave, and Amy asks if she can get a ride home from him. Tracey sits on the couch by the front window, peering through the curtains and watching the two of them walk to Frank's car, expecting to watch the usual puff of blue smoke coming out of Frank's tailpipe as he revs it up. What she sees instead is Amy and Frank making out. In a fit of rage, Tracey steals one of my mom's rings.

My mom confronts her the next day and Tracey denies stealing the ring, but my mom fires her anyway. Tracey starts babysitting for Billy's younger brother soon after; and to get back at her now ex-boyfriend Frank for his indiscretion with slutty big-boobed Amy, she sleeps with Billy's baseball-playing dad Larry one night after he offers to drive her home. Turns out, though, that Frank could care less about Tracey and Larry. He has fallen in love with Amy and her awesome breasts, and not necessarily in that order.

Larry accidentally gets Tracey pregnant, and she is sent away in secrecy to have the baby. Tracey refuses to tell anyone who the father is; but Larry's son Billy knows, because Billy was watching through the car window like normal. After this, Billy is no longer so obsessed with Amy's breasts. All he cares about now is avoiding Larry, and hurting himself whenever possible. He begins to take risks, sprinting across the freeway at night, cars missing him by a hair, jumping blindfolded off the old water-tower up on South Mountain into the bushes below, even drinking nail polish on a dare. Billy doesn't care about anything anymore, and why should he? The world is crazy and there's no making any sense of it.

One night at a party, Billy announces to no one in particular that he is going to do a cannonball into the empty pool in the backyard. Liz the crier grabs him by the arm and asks him to stop. Even though he doesn't know her that well, and barely remembers even fooling around with her, her dyed hair and goth clothing suits his mood; plus he's too drunk to resist, frankly. They sit by the edge of the pool and talk. "I hurt myself too," she says to him. "I cut myself. Little pricks across my arms, little slices across my thighs."

"Why?" Billy says. "Why would you do that?"

"It's the only thing that helps. It's just such a release from all the shit, you know?"

"I do know." He stares at her. He has fallen in love.

"I've done a terrible thing," Liz says, "and I've never told anyone, and it's killing me."

"I have a secret too," Billy says, "and I just want to run from it, and keep running, you know?"

"I do," Liz says. "So why not go, then, you and me? What do you say?"

And so they go. They leave that night and promise each other they will never come back. They can't, they claim—the neighborhood holds too many shadows for them.

People start whispering about Larry. *Did he or didn't he?* No one knows for sure, but they wonder. The wives stop sleeping with him, mumbling excuses about things "blowing over." With Tracey gone and having her baby, Amy with the boobs starts babysitting for Billy's little brother. Larry becomes transfixed with her, and decides he must have her. Amy is resistant, though; she's with Tracey's ex Frank now, is in love in fact, and besides has heard the whispers concerning Tracey's sudden "vacation" and Larry's possible involvement. Larry pushes and pushes the issue, though, asking again and again each time she babysits if he can make love to her at the end of the evening, never taking her protests seriously for even a moment. "C'mon, baby," he'd plead. "It'll be great. The best lay you ever had. Aren't you sick of those boys you've been sleeping with? Don't you want to know what it's like to be with a real man?" Amy can only resist so much. Eventually it becomes easier to just give in.

When her boyfriend Frank stops by her bedroom later that night, Amy is crying and won't tell him what happened. The next morning she is still crying, and Amy's parents ask her what's wrong as well. At first she is hesitant to say anything to them, but then says she will tell them what happened if they agree to leave the neighborhood. They do, and she does, and they leave the neighborhood soon thereafter. Amy tells Frank that she can't tell him what's gone on and can't look him in the face anymore either. She hopes that he does not hate her too much, and asks that he think of her always.

Frank of course can't think of anything else. He loves Amy and he wants answers. One night he goes by Larry's house with a case of beer and, as the night goes on, gets him to admit what happened. "Why don't you just tell me?" Frank says, after putting away eight or nine cans. "I know something happened, but she's gone now, you know? I mean, do you think I really fucking care at this point?"

"All right," Larry blearily says, as drunk that moment as Frank is. "I fucked her. I'm sorry. I did. But she wanted me, you know? What am I supposed to do? These women, these women out here, they just get their motors running, and suddenly there's nothing that can be done to stop them." Cracking open another beer, Larry proceeds to tell Frank all about Tracey and Liz and the dozens of other moms and daughters in the neighborhood he's slept with over the years. "It's beautiful in a way, actually," Larry says, pensively staring into the darkness beyond the porch. "All that joy I've spread."

Frank records the entire conversation, and after duping copies of the tape and slipping them into all the neighbors' mailboxes, heads out into the night in search of Amy, wherever she might now be. Larry's wife leaves him and takes their remaining son with her. The neighborhood dads stop coming around. Larry loses his swagger. He is alone now and without purpose. After awhile, he stops leaving the house and no one even seems to notice. The days, the months, and then even the years start to pass. One day with the mail piling up and the lawn overgrown, the police kick in Larry's door. They find him dead on the living-room floor, surrounded by garbage, piles of old newspapers, and Pirates memorabilia.

And me, I never leave the neighborhood. I don't see any reason to. It's quiet and I like it that way. I stay long enough, in fact, to watch everyone eventually move back. First it is Amy and Frank; turns out he actually managed to track her down, and one thing led to another, and Frank never really wanted to leave in the first place, which is why they came back here. Billy and Liz then drifted in sometime after that; they've been all around the country, they say, but never found what they thought they were looking for, never found the inner peace they thought that distance would bring them. Even Tracey comes back—she is alone, childless and with no explanation of what happened, but she seems happy and who are we to doubt her? Once in awhile we all get together at someone's house and barbecue some steaks. We have a couple of beers, we laugh, and we shoot the shit. It's nice.

The Gift

FERN LIKED MOTORCYCLE BOOTS, black and scuffed, and she liked to wear them with long flowing skirts. She liked her brown hair short, with a slight part to the side, a few spare tendrils sneaking out behind her ears. She rarely wore makeup, but liked to pluck her eyebrows, the better for raising them Belushi-style when feigning surprise, awe, or self-mockery. She liked Hello Kitty. And the band Cake. She liked the movie *Mermaids* so much she saw it seven times. She never drank or smoked, but she liked nothing more than shooting pool in dark, musty bars. She hated George Bush, people who neglected to screw the top back on tubes of toothpaste, and the fact that she failed to put her sunglasses in the same place every time she removed them. She favored tank-tops and long leather jackets, but always wore a formal gown when watching the Oscars. She abhorred violence and injustice of all kinds, but especially against women. She was a leader in the student protests against admitting men to Mills College, and once traveled across Nicaragua on a rusty bike. She liked folktales and storytelling and had once created a video installation of three couples tickling each other—the sounds of their breath, their skin-on-skin contact, and their laughter reverberating across the abandoned warehouse where the work was first shown. Mostly, though, Fern liked sound, all kinds of sound, and her inability to block out the sounds that surrounded her, a trait she was sure was a gift bestowed on her from some higher power.

As a child, Fern would spend all afternoon sitting in front of the washing machines at the neighborhood laundromat listening to the *shwap, shwap, shwap* of the water sloshing about, the blades spinning, the socks and underwear crashing into one another. She would lay in the endless fields behind the neighborhood church and listen to the landscaping crew for hours, the tinny whine of the lawnmower motor and the occasional ping of a rock getting caught underneath it, bringing her great pleasure and solace. The plucky chirps of birds were forever entertaining to her…as were barking dogs, the beeps and whistles of trucks backing into driveways, the rain slapping a staccato beat against the windows of her classrooms at school, and the *swack, swack, swack* of the baseball cards the boys next door attached to the wheels of their bikes.

In comparison, home was no place to be. It was noiseless and unbearable. No one spoke at meals. And no one asked about one another's day, much less about how they might be feeling. Worse though, there was no place in her home to hide or go that was far enough away to escape the crushing quiet, the fears that accompanied it, or the long nights Fern spent staring at the tiles on her bedroom ceiling, ten rows across, fifteen rows down, 150 total, 75 white, 75 black, 25 of which were cracked.

But the sounds that engulfed her outside of her home, these she could hide in, and revel in, creating a world that was hers and hers alone. Sound made sense; it provided her with both an anchor and a lifeline. Sound could be classified, explained, and organized, whereas regular life could not. It was too messy and unpredictable. People came and went, emotions changed from one moment to the next, relationships were unmanageable, and Fern wanted nothing to do with this. She wanted to feel something, and be excited by something, and discovering new sounds provided her with this. With sound came purpose, and with purpose the world finally made sense.

While Fern was all about collecting sound, however, she never did so in a systematic way; she simply left the house and went somewhere, and she savored what awaited her. This changed, though, when she left Two Rivers and moved to the city. There were all sorts of new sounds to discover here—the rattling of the Seven train as it emerged into the light of Long Island City, the whoosh the steam produced as it mysteriously arose from the sidewalk grates, the reverberations the escalators made as you descended into Penn Station on the Madison Square Garden side of the building. It was a whole new world and Fern embraced it lovingly, and ferociously.

It was around this time that Fern decided to start recording the sounds she loved so much. She bought little tape recorders that she attached to her feet so she could capture the resulting *crunch, crunch, crunch* as she walked through the day-old snow in Central Park; and then later slipped them into her pockets while on the Three train, so she could record random snippets of conversation as she came home from her job as an administrative assistant, to a realtor off of Broadway and West 35th:

So you slept with her?
Yeah.
Are you going to tell your wife?
No. I don't want to hurt her.
That's very generous of you.
I think so.

I met Fern at the Dive Bar up on Amsterdam. I was simply looking to shoot some darts and drink some beer; but there she was, sitting by herself in the back, nursing some seltzer water, a little smile on her face. I wouldn't normally approach someone like that, someone so clearly happy to be by themselves; but that smile, it was different, enigmatic. I had to know what was behind it.

"Anyone sitting here?" I asked.

No, she said, then held up a finger. One minute. She reached under the table and produced a tape recorder that she promptly turned off. She jotted some commentary into a little notebook and then turned her attention to me.

"What are you doing?" I said.

"Capturing bar sounds," she said. "You know—bottles crashing into one another, pool balls ricocheting from one to the next, small talk, people washing dirty glasses."

"Why?" I said, now smiling myself.

"Because it makes me happy," she said.

We got pizza at La Famiglia at the corner of 96th, bought some beers at the bodega around the corner, and went back to her place, a little studio apartment in a building down by the West Side Highway. The room was dominated by two things—a futon bed, and shelf after shelf of tapes divided into bizarre, random-sounding sections, all of them labeled with yellowing masking tape:

Dogs (big)
Dogs (small)
Bus announcements
Horses (hansom cabs)

At some point while we were listening, I drifted off, and when I awoke the next morning I was surrounded by open tape boxes and

Fern was making us pancakes.

After that I joined her in her work. I was expected to come up with ideas, note locations where I heard especially anomalous sounds, and help Fern with her equipment and set-up when she was ready to record. At times she produced detailed schedules and maps about our plans for the day, and at other times we just wandered, knowing we would eventually stumble onto something we were both captivated by. We captured the roar of the fans at Yankee Stadium; the din created by the big machines at Staten Island construction sites; the whir of the mammogram she took after she found a lump one morning in the shower. We were on a grand adventure, a search for sound in all of its forms, colors, tastes, and smells. We talked about building some kind of archive on the internet and writing little stories to accompany our efforts.

"Can you feel it?" Fern would say again and again.

"What?" I would always reply.

"We're doing something great here," she would say.

"We are?" I would reply.

"Of course we are," she would say. "We're creating something bigger than ourselves, something that will outlive us."

"Why do you even care about that?" I would reply. "You're 25 years old."

"It's never too soon to think about your legacy," she would say. "Don't you want to leave some kind of mark that you were here?"

"I guess," I would reply. "But what about children? Won't they be your legacy?"

"I'm not having children," she would say. "There's too much pain in the world."

"How can you of all people say that?" I would reply. "Look at this amazing thing you're doing. Look at how much pleasure it brings you."

"Yes, but there's no guarantee that my kids would find something they love, to fill whatever hole they find themselves in," she would say. "And I don't want the responsibility for having to worry about that. Now enough of this. What should we tackle today?"

One day she had this idea that she would ride her bike to work, her tape recorders capturing the sounds of the trip—the people rushing to the office, the car horns and vendors, the dogs barking, the police blowing their whistles, the flapping of her long skirt as the wind washed across her legs, a grown-up version of the baseball cards from the neighbors' bikes of her childhood. I called her at work later that morning, hoping to find out what she had recorded, wondering when I might be able to hear the results. She wasn't at work, though; she had never come in, actually, and she had never called. Nor was she at home. No one knew where she was. I went to her apartment at the end of the day and saw Fern's landlord by her door.

"Did you know her?" the landlord asked me. He was a bald guy in a wifebeater and blue Dickies.

"Yes," I said. "Why?"

"She was run over by a bus on her way to work today," he said. "Got her skirt caught in the chain of her bike. It's a shame. She was funny. An unusual kid."

There was a memorial service for Fern and then her family took her home to be buried. And now I think of her every single time it rains here in the city, every single time some car slams on its brakes. But I also think about her when nothing is happening at all—no movement, no sound, just silence, profound and sublime silence. She wouldn't have understood it, but she would have appreciated it, I think, finding something in nothing, something wonderful to immerse yourself in when pain is the only other option. She knew how important that kind of thing could be.

What We Thought We Knew

THESE WERE THE FACTS about Lacey Chalmers as we understood them. She had short blonde hair, long skinny legs, green eyes, and shoulders that were perpetually slumped forward because she was embarrassed about her height. She had non-existent breasts, was a solid but unremarkable member of the varsity volleyball team, and had a smile that would sometimes come out of nowhere and suddenly light up a room. She wasn't cute per se, and she wasn't not cute either; she was what she was, and I guess for the most part we just didn't really ever think about her that way.

Lacey's birth had not been planned, and her parents were not young. Her father Frank was in his sixties when she was born, and her mother Annie was in her forties. They had not intended to have children, and really didn't even sleep together any more, except for the occasional birthday or anniversary celebration. Frank, however, had been regularly banging his youngish overtall blonde secretary Mary, and had gotten her pregnant. Mary did not want to keep the baby, but Annie talked Frank into talking Mary into having it. "I want to raise it as our own," she said to Frank, in a way that made it clear that he had no right at this point to argue.

Lacey was in the Key Club and a member of the honor society. She had her heart set on attending Williams College and had no second choice in mind. Lacey and Frank played golf together on the public course twice a month when the weather was good, and Lacey and Annie watched the movie *Mermaids* together over and over again. While Frank may have had moments when he resented having Lacey around as a reminder of the things he wished he had not done, and while Annie may have kind of wanted to raise Lacey for just that very reason, it was still a happy, quiet house, where people went about their business undisturbed.

Lacey would have dated more, but people didn't really ask her. She did have her admirers though. There was Ted, for example—he of the perpetually bad skin, bad hair, and Harvard ambitions. Ted didn't get out much, and while it was clear that this was due in part to his study habits, as well as his penchant for Dungeons and Dragons, the fact was his family was unusually close and his father Jonathan liked to have Ted and his brothers in the house doing family things when he wasn't at work. This seemed odd to the rest of us—no one's family spent that much time together—but Jonathan was from Australia and none of us knew how they operated down there.

When we were eight, and long before I had begun to truly worry about being cool, much less being around those I perceived to be cool, Ted invited me to sleep over at his house. We didn't spend that much time together, but the fact that he had just received a copy of the new Asteroids cartridge for his Atari trumped everything else, and we played until our thumbs were swollen and our eyes were blurry. At some point Jonathan told us it was time to go to bed, and after Ted kissed Jonathan on the cheek I started to follow him upstairs. Jonathan—who had pale blotchy skin and thin wispy hair that hung across his face—looked at me, looked at Ted, and then smiled and said, "No one goes to bed in this house without first giving me a kiss goodnight."

If I paused, it was brief. Of course the request seemed odd to me, because it was Ted's dad asking for a kiss and not, say, Ted's mom, who you never saw much of anyway. But at that age, I would never have seriously questioned an adult's overtures of any kind; it would never even have occurred to me to do so. I quickly kissed Jonathan on the cheek, and the oddness passed. The next morning, when my dad came to pick me up and asked me how the sleepover had gone, I didn't say anything to him about kissing Jonathan goodnight. I didn't say anything at all really, but it didn't matter, because he was already thinking about other things.

"I like a family that spends time together," he said, "and I like seeing a father who seems to value that." I didn't respond to that either; our family didn't spend that much time together, and it was safe to say that wasn't going to change any time soon. Then again, what did I know about parents? Nothing. They lived in a different world than we did. I never slept at Ted's again, though, but then again never planned it on purpose either. At some point I think he just stopped inviting people to stay over, and if that is true it didn't matter to any of us anyway, not really. Ted wasn't that cool, and we were finally old enough that that mattered.

What we also knew was that Ted was in love with Lacey, and while she tried to keep her distance, he knew that after he convinced her to go to the prom with him she would love him as well. In fact, Ted was so sure they would end up together, he had already memorized the directions between Harvard and Williams because he also knew that he was going to be making that drive quite often. The way Ted envisioned it, if he could find a good-enough route, he'd be able to make it to Lacey's campus late on Friday afternoons, right before rush-hour started, and if she had a class he could just wait for her at the student union and do his schoolwork. When she was ready they would go have an early dinner before heading back to her room, where they would spend the rest of the weekend together lying in bed, reading, writing long romantic letters to each other and making love.

Ted knew these things would happen, because he knew that nobody understood Lacey like he did. Certainly no one had studied her quite like he had, but that made sense because no one else felt about her quite like he did either. For example, did anyone else know that she was obsessed with Barry Manilow and that she drew his picture over and over again when she was upset about something? Probably not, but they probably hadn't watched her during study-hall quite as intensely as he had. Did anyone else know the route she took to get home from school, the exact route, including the walls she walked along, the backyards she cut through, and the bushes she jumped over? Definitely not, but who else had repeatedly followed her home, from a safe distance of course? No one, that's who, nor did anyone else know that late at night, when everyone else was asleep, she violently danced to the Ramones in front of her bedroom window. But how could they? How many of them had actually witnessed it?

Ted had never even kissed Lacey, but he knew he would, because while Ted had never discussed the prom with her, he knew it was just a matter of time before he did. And once he did, he knew Lacey would go with him, they were meant to be together, and that he knew without a doubt.

One night there was a party at Johanna Levy's house. Johanna's parents were never home on the weekends; it was something you could count on like clockwork. You also knew you could always count on someone's older brother or sister buying you beer; and that at some point the combination of the party and the alcohol would provide you with the chance to hook up with someone. There might only prove to be a small window of opportunity to do so, but there would definitely be one at some point, something we knew to be true, regardless of how successful we actually were.

Oddly enough, Lacey was at Johanna's that night. They were not friends, but they were neighbors, all the way back from being kids, and nothing particularly negative had ever occurred between them. Like Ted and I, Johanna and Lacey had gone off in different directions at some point; you weren't sure why, but you knew that Lacey was Lacey, that she wasn't that cool, so you knew it had something to do with that even if you didn't exactly want to admit to it.

When I first saw Lacey she was at the keg. We were not that friendly, but we weren't unfriendly, and she always had a smile for me. "Hey," she said a little unsteadily. "It's going to be my birthday at midnight."

"No shit," I said. "Great. Happy birthday."

"Yeah," she said, nodding to the music and looking down at her cup. "So, you know, maybe you'll give me a kiss at midnight?"

"Um, sure," I said, taken aback for a moment. "Anything you want."

"Cool, cool," she said, still nodding, suddenly walking away without saying anything else.

She was joking, of course, had to be, or else was so wasted she would never actually remember the conversation by the time midnight rolled around; I didn't even consider actually kissing her later. But I would, I definitely would if she wanted to, if she asked me in a way that was real, that she would remember.

At midnight I felt a tap on my shoulder. It was Lacey. "You didn't think I was joking, did you?"

"Kind of. We barely ever speak."

"And who's fault is that?" she said. We remained silent for a moment, then she said, "Are you going to kiss me?"

I leaned in towards her and she responded in kind. Her lips were warm, electric, like fresh fruit. We started to kiss, slowly, softly, then faster, and harder. I pushed into her and she moved with me. I buried my hands in her hair and she grabbed my neck, pulling me closer to her, and then closer still. I paused, panicked by the intensity. I pulled back. She smiled.

"Thank you," she said, walking away.

And that was the moment I became a lifelong admirer of Lacey, though always from afar, too scared to know what to do about it.

Lacey had one other admirer as well—Mr. Elmo, the music teacher who was youngish and desperate to be hip, with his longish prog-rock hair and tasteful little beard. He was married to an even younger woman of indeterminate Asian descent, who never left their little house and was rumored to hand-stitch his mainly hemp clothes. It was said that they spent their weekends getting together with faculty couples from the local college, getting high, watching porn, and swapping wives. But no one could confirm this. What we could confirm was that Mr. Elmo's slightly pudgy frame sweated a lot, and we knew this because each and every time we had music class, we would have to watch his hand-stitched hemp clothes became saturated over the course of an hour.

We also knew, or thought we knew, that he seemed to like young girls. And it wasn't because he clearly smiled more when they raised their hands, or that he liked to rub their shoulders during class, or even how he was forever offering the girls rides home from school in his beat-up VW Karmann Ghia, because he just happened to be going that way. No, it was the way he looked at them when they didn't know it, like a panhandler staring through the window of a restaurant at a hot, open-faced turkey sandwich. There was a raw hunger in his eyes when he thought no one was looking; a desperate, churning desire to devour the girls in one big cartoonish bite.

And we knew, at least heard anyway, that Mr. Elmo had been asked to leave other schools for exactly this kind of stuff, and that his wife was in fact a former student of his, a woman who had gone on to be a student-teacher and then found her first husband in bed with another man. Everyone knew this, it was the word around school; and if the information wasn't entirely accurate, there was certainly no one around who could dispute it either.

Of course, that was what we thought we knew. What we didn't know is that Lacey had slept with Mr. Elmo. It had happened on a class trip to Quebec that Mr. Elmo had chaperoned. Mr. Elmo had plied her with her raspberry wine coolers one night and told her how beautiful she was, had told her that he was lonely and that his wife didn't understand him or his dreams of being a full-time musician, his dreams of getting out of this endless rut of teaching a bunch of sullen spoiled teens who don't give a shit about art or beauty or truth.

Lacey was impressed, and admitted that her parents didn't understand her either, slurring as she related their latest argument. "'Why do you need to go all the way to Williams?' they say. 'Why not stay with us? We love you. Aren't we all happy here? Why ruin that?' But that's exactly why I want to go away. I feel smothered."

"I know, I know," Mr. Elmo said. "Like, just loving someone isn't enough. They need to understand your dreams as well, and support those dreams. Without that, how can you even call it love?"

"Yeah, totally," Lacey said. "You really get me, don't you?"

"I do," Mr. Elmo said, opening another two wine coolers. "I really do."

Moments after they were done having sex, Mr. Elmo said, "You better leave my room now."

"Don't you want me here?"

"Sure I do. But I'm a chaperone and you're a student." He ran his fingers down her cheek. "You don't want me to get in trouble, do you?" And she didn't, and so she left.

The next day, when Lacey tried to walk with Mr. Elmo through the local History Of Labor Museum, he kept finding various ways to ensure that the two were never left alone. It remained this way for the rest of the trip, and when returning home the incident was never spoken about again.

While we did not know that Lacey had slept with Mr. Elmo, what we also didn't know was that Ted had gone on the trip to Quebec to be near Lacey, that he had followed Lacey to Mr. Elmo's room, listening to all that had gone down. Nor did we know how much rage Ted felt about life in general those days—that he cut himself regularly, tortured small animals, wrote stories of mutilation and violence that he feverishly hid away in a box under his bed. If we had known this, we might not have been so surprised when eventually learning that Ted burned down Mr. Elmo's house. But we didn't know these things, just like we didn't know why Ted's Australian father was so gung-ho on being inside the house with his sons all the time. We didn't know that he had been sexually abusing them for years. We didn't know such things even happened. Not really, anyway.

And the fact that Ted was essentially let off on juvenile probation; the fact that Mr. Elmo and his wife quietly moved away a few weeks later; the fact that Ted's father permanently left the country the year after that; the fact that Lacey did not get into Williams after all; none of that seemed to mean all that much when everything was said and done. What we thought we knew wasn't very important, because the fact was that we didn't know shit, and you never do.

Change of Plans

I'M HOME FOR THE SUMMER, so my uncle finagles me a job with the pipeline maintenance crew at Susquehanna Gas, four full-timers with little to do and even less supervision. There's Ethan, an older guy, who has a second career as a sustenance farmer at his home, just playing out another four years on the city payroll until his pension kicks in; he's the first one to unbutton his pants after lunch, the first to suggest we take it easy instead of doing work. Then there's Wyatt— he's wiry, lives on black coffee, and talks endlessly about whatever pops into his head, regardless of whether it's accurate or not...

"I don't think that you boys quite appreciate the benefits of a high caffeine level in the bloodstream."

"Is that right, Wyatt. Well, why don't you illuminate us."

"First off, if you drink coffee all day, it keeps you sharp, so you don't need as much sleep, and you can get more done. Second, it dehydrates you, so while you don't have to waste as much time taking a piss, it still ensures regular bowel movements. And finally, it fills you up and you don't feel like snacking as much. The result? No wasted calories."

"Jesus Christ, Wyatt. Will you please shut the fuck up."

There's also Boone; a handsome guy, in his early thirties I think, who has a house he's constantly working on, and a former-cheerleader wife who all the other guys call a surprisingly nice piece of ass when he isn't around; and then finally there's Bill, stringy-haired and odd, who will go huge periods of time saying nothing and then suddenly pipe up with something outrageously inappropriate.

The guys all like to joke around, and they all like to talk a lot of shit:

Ethan: "The wife's losing interest in me, you know. She's got grandchildren now; what the hell does she need me for? I may just need to move on."

Wyatt: "Maybe you could trade her in for a new one, like you did with that old tractor of yours."

Boone: [Laughter] "Maybe you could find yourself a little something on the side, like a farmer's daughter."

Bill: "Maybe you could fuck one of your goats."

[Silence.]

Ethan: "What the fuck is wrong with you, Bill?"

Most days that summer follow the same pattern: we start by all rolling in around 9:30 or so, and spending the morning lazily idling around the concrete garage the crew calls home, drinking coffee and reading the paper and shooting the shit. Then around 10:30, 11, we'll finally get out and work for an hour or two—cleaning brush, surveying a new sewer line. A two-hour break for lunch; then back to the garage for a game of cards and more chit-chat; then another hour or two of work in the afternoon; and then it's back home usually around 4:30.

One day near the end of work, Boone asks if I can head back

to his place with him for a little bit, help him out with a two-man project in return for some beer and steaks. I say sure and we go and grab one of the dump-trucks from the parking lot. We head to the quarry, where Boone picks up a load of rocks. "I'm building a patio in my backyard, he says, and I want to lay down some rocks before I pour the concrete." After leaving the quarry we head to Boone's house, out on the edge of nowhere like so much of Two Rivers is, where he proceeds to dump the rocks in a big pile in his backyard. We start shoveling and raking, shoveling and raking.

A couple of minutes in, Boone wipes his brow and yells out, "Hon? Could you grab us a couple of beers?" I hear a faint "Sure," and a moment later, his wife Kristy comes out. She's wearing cutoff jeans and a t-shirt with a country-music star on it, and I can see why the other guys on the crew say the things they do when Boone isn't around.

"Thanks, baby," Boone says, taking the bottles from her and handing one to me. "This is the summer guy down at work I was telling you about."

Kristy stares into my eyes and smiles. Her pupils are an impossibly light green, like sparkling emeralds that hypnotize you with their shininess. "Nice to meet you," she says.

"I...nice...it's," I stumble. "It's nice to meet you too."

She turns back to Boone. "When you going to be done with all this, you think?"

"Well, I gotta get the truck back tonight, then I'll probably stop off at Thirsty's for a bit." He shrugs. "Late evening?"

"Not too late. I want to talk to you about something."

"All right, all right," he says, smooching her on the cheek as she walks back into the house. "Nice to meet you," she calls out again over her shoulder before disappearing.

Boone silently watches her go in, then sighs. "A little advice," he says, still looking back at the house. "Don't marry the first girl willing to give you a blowjob and swallow." Then he chuckles, so I do too, and we take drinks from our beers, and then he mutters, "She wants to talk to me about something. Are you fucking kidding me." He puts his bottle down, shaking his head, and we get back to work.

After bringing the truck back to the maintenance compound, we indeed stop by Thirsty's for a couple of pitchers. It's a dark, damp place, murkily lit by a series of neon beer ads scattered throughout, half-filled on any given night with grizzled locals. Soon Boone is adding tequila shots to the affair, and then he's buying shots for a couple of the women who are there alone on a Thursday night, and then one of them is suddenly at the table with us, Cindy Who Likes The Bills which is about the only thing that permeates my drunken, fuzzy brain. And then the next thing I know, Boone's saying something about how he's going to catch a ride with her instead, and leaving yet another twenty for me to stay and enjoy myself. And I'm suddenly sitting with yet another beer in front of me, looking at a poster on the wall and thinking how there's something seriously wrong with the concept of talking lizards selling alcohol.

And then suddenly Kristy's there beside me, shaking my shoulder and saying, "Hello? I said, have you seen Boone?" She's changed outfits, now with teased-out hair and a low-cut v-neck t-shirt.

"Oh," I say, my eyes focusing. "Sorry. Sorry. Boone. Um. Yeah. He was. Um. Here."

She looks at me silently, nodding imperceptibly and with her lips pursed. "I see," she says. "And then he left." It's more of a statement than a question.

"Um, yeah. And then he left."

She looks around the room, sighs, then looks back at me. "Well," she says, "why don't I give you a ride home at least? You don't look like you're in much of a position to drive."

"Sure," I say, getting up and wobbling just a bit less than I was expecting to. "Sure."

We drive up Pennsylvania Avenue, veering off onto Morgan Road, past Ross Park Zoo, before continuing on until we reach Mill Hill, a stretch of empty road just a few turns away from where I live. Kristy pulls over and kills the lights. It's dark up here and desolate; no housing, no cars, no streetlights or trees, just the top of a hill, and a whole lot of nothing. "Can I ask you a question?" she says.

"Yes."

"Today. At the house. Was your stammering because of me?" I look down at my lap and laugh, embarrassed. She smiles. "Do you have a girlfriend back at school?"

"No, ma'am."

She winces. "Please. It's Kristy."

"Um. No. Kristy."

"Have you ever thought about." She pauses. "Being with someone older than you?"

The air inside the car is getting stuffy and oppressive, the windows starting to steam. "I've thought about it," I say. "Yeah, sure, I've thought about it."

"And what did you think?" She leans in just a little closer to me.

I pause for a long time, looking at the ceiling of the car's cabin and trying to figure out what to say; but before I can respond, she's already started smiling and saying, "Actually, okay, you just told me." She bends over to dig through her purse, pulls out one of those thin chick cigarettes and lights it. She leans back, takes a long drag and exhales, looking at me silently for a moment, then finally turns back to the wheel. "Well," she says, starting up the engine again. "Let's get you home, huh?"

The next day at work I try to avoid Boone, but it's hard when it's just a five-man crew and you spend most of your day together in a little concrete garage. Over a round of Hearts and a fresh pot of coffee that afternoon, he says, "So I guess Kristy and you ran into each other last night."

"Um, yeah," I say, staring at my cards. "That's right."

He nods, looking at his cards as well. "Appreciate you not blabbing about me buying all those drinks for Cindy. I hate it when a man steps into another man's business like that."

I shrug. "I barely remember. I was wasted."

"Yep, yep." He lays down a card, starting a new round. "One thing I can't stand, it's guys getting into other guys' business. Don't you agree, Ethan?" Boone's still staring at his cards, not looking at any of us. "Don't you agree, for example, a man deserves to be punished for fucking around with another man's wife?"

"Hmm?" Ethan looks up from his own cards, confused. "Oh, I don't care. Maybe I'd be grateful to get my wife off my hands at this point."

Bill slaps down the Queen of Spades. "Or you could just kill her," he says, "then leave the body in that giant compost heap of yours until it turns into mulch."

They all stop and look in his direction. Squinting his eyes, Boone says, "Bill, what the fuck is wrong with you?"

And then that's it; suddenly the summer is over, and I'm heading back to school, a few thousand dollars richer and with a newfound appreciation for black coffee. And, you know, I never did get to see how that patio ended up turning out.

Pac-Man Fever

I MET GEORGE IN SCHOOL. He was always a little pasty, all the way through childhood, and had a habit of wearing the same pants for sometimes three or four days in a row, usually a series of interchangeable brown and blue and gray corduroys. George had a look of defeat about him from the first day I met him, like a guy who had hit the game-winning triple only to get tagged out because he failed to touch second base. His mom Kim had been a school lunch monitor when we were kids. She was partial to polyester pantsuits and big hair, but she was funny, and "earthy" as my mom liked to say, and she never failed to have any number of young guys around her when she and her friends went out to Thirsty's for drinks.

If this bothered George's dad Starnsey, he never said. Nor did he say anything much when Kim left home with Ray, the manager of the garage down the street. One day she was there, and the next day she wasn't. But Starnsey never said a word about it, and so neither did George. George wondered why Kim might want to leave, but it seemed pointless to ask Starnsey about it; he just wasn't that type. And so they went about their business, like all was normal, like there was nothing odd about one day your mom being there and one day not.

Kim and Starnsey had met when she came into the little convenience store he owned, to buy a pack of cigarettes. It had been a whirlwind romance—a weeklong courtship, an impromptu wedding before the justice of the peace, a two-day honeymoon in Niagara Falls, and George's birth nine months to the day of the wedding. It had started off well enough, but it was fast, and what Kim couldn't have known of course was that Starnsey was prone to dark stretches of incapacitating depression, times when he could do little more then sit behind the counter of the store if he could in fact get out of bed at all.

At first Kim tried to make it all work—caring for Starnsey, caring for George, getting a job at the school, running the store at night as needed. And for a year or two this was okay, and even year three wasn't terrible, but when year four rolled around and George became yet more demanding, Kim began to wonder where her youth had gone and why she had let go of it so readily. Soon there were drinks after work and minor flirtations. And then there were drinks followed by furtive sexual encounters in her car, outside the Pine Lounge and in the alley behind Thirsty's.

And then there was Ray. With his bushy mustache and bowlegged gait, he was handsome in an urban-cowboy kind of way. He was also young and in love, and only too happy to be told what to do. When he promised Kim a better life, she saw an out and she took it. They headed to Florida and then Houston, going wherever there was steady work and a steady supply of alcohol. At first, George heard from Kim every once in awhile, and then not at all; it was just George and Starnsey now, and that wasn't much.

With Kim gone, Starnsey became even more reclusive—her

loss had aged him, and without her to care for him, his bouts with depression became longer and more tortured. Starnsey would become unable to leave his bed for days, if not weeks, at a time. He couldn't cook for either himself or George, or even make himself get up to bathe more than once a week or so. George became Starnsey's full-time caretaker, and by the time we reached the ninth grade George had stopped attending school. He tended to Starnsey, tended to the store and made time for little else.

And so it went until something amazing happened—Pudgie's Pizza opened up down the street from Starnsey's store. Where once there was nowhere to go when school and homework and sports were done, we now had a destination, a place of our own away from adults and rules. You could get two plain slices of pizza and a small soda for 99 cents, a dozen chicken wings for two dollars, and an order of deep-fried mushrooms with Russian dressing on the side for a buck twenty-five. You could also play this bizarre new videogame called Pac-Man, a game that was such a departure from the simplistic, war-based, one-dimensional, black-and-white games we had been used to up to that point.

The game cost a quarter. It had multiple colors and a soundtrack. The game was comprised of a maze filled with white dots. The goal was for the Pac-Man—a little yellow circle with a notch cut for a mouth—to consume the dots while being chased by four ghosts, gremlin-like creatures that were either red, blue, yellow, or green, and that roamed the maze all obsessed like Dirty Harry with one mission and one mission only—catch and kill the Pac-Man. The dots were each worth points and in each corner of the maze were larger dots that when consumed allowed the Pac-Man for a short time period to consume the ghosts, the hunted briefly allowed to become the hunter.

You controlled the Pac-Man's direction by a knob on the machine, and for the most part you yanked it around and mindlessly cruised the maze as long as you could, tempting death, hoping for inspiration, and trying to avoid capture. When all the dots on the screen were consumed, you moved on to the next level, where the ghosts became even faster, and if you could get through that level, another one awaited, that was faster still, and on and on you went until all your Pac-Men were dead. You were on your own in there, but as far as we knew the game was endless, and as long as you could stay alive the levels would continue on into infinity. Or at least, we could never imagine anyone getting a score high enough to actually "break" the machine's scoring system.

We played endlessly, spending our allowance and lawnmowing money while it lasted, and then our lunch money, and then our old birthday money we had been saving, and finally the money we would filch from our fathers' pants pockets and mothers' pocketbooks as they slept. The top-ten scores list changed constantly as we all tried to master the game, and we all had those moments where nothing went wrong, where the Pac-Man was always a little faster than the ghosts and our vision transcended our more earthbound constraints. No one played more or worked harder then George, though, and no one could compete with him.

It wasn't just that he could play during the day while we were at school, or that he didn't have a curfew, or even that he had an unlimited supply of quarters from the store, though these things all helped; it was just that George simply wanted it more than we did. Unlike his home life, which was confusing and messy, Pac-Man had clear boundaries and rules. You followed a defined path, and though you were being chased the whole time, if you were smart, and played within yourself, you could achieve liberation and greatness. It was black and white and George craved that; it spoke to him and he embraced it like a lover to his beloved, after returning home from a long journey.

George was something to watch too. He was like a rockstar up there, a cigarette in one hand, the knob in the other, surrounded by the neon signs advertising Bud Light, breathlessly eluding the ghosts, eating dots, and marching through one board after another. George had a swagger at the machine that he possessed in no other facet of his life. George was the king and not only did he have little intention of abdicating his throne, he knew he would never have to. We were all competing for second place, and we accepted that. We were in the presence of greatness.

At first George was merely a phenom, a freak—a player gifted with quick wrists, concentration, vision, and fearlessness. Soon, though, he made an important discovery; the game was less random then we all thought. The ghosts did not merely follow the Pac-Man around the board, but were programmed to follow certain paths in certain ways; and while they responded to your decisions about where the Pac-Man should go next, if you studied their reactions it soon became obvious how they would respond, and which direction they would go.

Armed with such insights a person could set the pace, go on the offensive, and ultimately conquer the game. When George realized this, his focus on the game moved from obsession to compulsion. He began to study every move and its subsequent ramifications. He started to show up when Pudgie's opened its doors and stay until closing, only breaking long enough to run home and care for Starnsey or manage the store during the rare busy stretches of the day. Otherwise, it was all about the game—learning it, living it, making it his own.

We watched and watched as George became the master of this small slice of the universe. Once there, it didn't matter that his mom had left or that his father was often in a catatonic state; he was a magician weaving a spell that we all found ourselves captivated by. Soon the question was not whether George could conquer the machine, but when he would, and what it would look like and what would happen afterwards. This was before the internet, remember; although there had been a series of urban rumors whispered in the arcades about this kid or another reaching a fabled "final level," of unlocking an entire sequence of new animations once beating that final board, none of us among the "Pudgie's crowd" had ever actually seen such a miracle for ourselves.

But one night, though, we finally found out. Like usual, none of us even paid attention to the first 50 screens or so, George passing through them with the contempt that befits a champion destroying a lesser opponent. It was like Bird playing a game against the Clippers; showing up is required, but there's no real reason to break a sweat. George kept going and going, though, and we all took notice. Screen after screen disappeared before us, as George seemed to drift further and further away; he was in the zone, oblivious to anything but the game.

Thirty minutes passed and George was still going. Then 45 minutes. And then an hour. George was soon up to level 200, down to his last Pac-Man, with still no end in sight and no one quite sure how much longer the game would last. He took a bite of pizza, a sip of coke, and pushed on, a cigarette always burning in his left hand. And then suddenly it was level 256, and although the game itself was behaving the same as always, the entire right-half of the maze was now filled with random garbage, computing gobblety-gook, which of course made it almost impossible to play, because you couldn't see what you were doing or where the ghosts were or how many dots were left or anything. And sure enough, George's last Pac-Man died a quick and ignoble death, and then there was nothing; no special lights or bells, no bikini-clad models pouring champagne or giving George a kiss, just a return to the top-ten list, and George's score of 3,300,100, and a prompt for his initials.

So George added his usual gaming nom-de-plume, VHX ("Van Halen Rox"), calmly walked away from the machine, sat down at a booth and finished his cold pizza. He drank some more soda and had another cigarette. He looked lost and worn out, and not at all triumphant as one might have hoped.

"So is that all there is?" he tiredly asked me.

"Yeah, I guess."

"I'm not sure what to do now."

"Savor it, motherfucker." I shrugged. "Enjoy it. Do it again."

He sighed. "Sure, okay," he said, getting up. "I gotta go check on my pops. See you later."

The next morning I woke up to the dog barking like crazy in the backyard. I walked out there half-convinced that I'd find George hanging from a tree, pale and not moving, his hair damp from the morning dew, his lips a ghostly blue. But George wasn't out there, just some baby birds hopping around and squawking, waiting for their mother to return home with their breakfast.

I didn't see much of George after that; he never really came back to Pudgie's, and in fact never left Starnsey's much at all. I think he's still there, but I haven't checked to find out. It's too sad a story for me—a god falls to earth, and all he has to show for it are three initials on a videogame screen.

Life As He Had Known It

IT HAD BEEN MOVING SO FAST, Matt thought. It had been time to have a baby; both he and Sheila had agreed on that. But then suddenly she was pregnant. They had known it might take awhile and Matt was okay with that, but it hadn't—two months, boom, she felt different, she peed on a stick, and there they were. Soon a month had passed, then two; one trimester begat a second. There were names to be picked, and strollers, classes on breastfeeding and infant CPR.

Bob, the guy who taught the infant CPR class, was a hulk—his enormous shoulders straining the sleeves of his polo shirt, his thick thighs packed into his khakis like sausages, his hands the biggest Matt had ever seen, like pink fleshy waffle irons. "Let me just tell you folks something right off the bat," Bob said. "You will probably never need to use a single technique I am going to teach you today. The fact that you're here shows you care enough to pay attention to your child."

And Matt hoped that was true, because ten minutes after the class ended Matt couldn't remember a thing. Then again, he couldn't remember much of anything these days; life was just flying by, all of it, all of it was a blur. And then suddenly it wasn't. They started getting things done and life began to move at half-speed. The crib was ordered and the baby's windows were sealed. Names were chosen— Fiona if it was a girl and Charlie if it was a boy. Blood kits obtained. Bags packed, including a pair of shorts for Matt, who was reminded by a nurse that he was not allowed to lounge around the hospital without pants on, as some new fathers were wont to do.

There was nothing left to work on, and so Matt caught his breath and focused on things he had not been able to get to before. He filed some papers that had been piling up on his desk—bank notices and pay stubs, health insurance updates and reports on the status of his 401k. He caught up on the back issues of The New Yorker that had been piling up. He handed off what he could at work and watched the complete first season of *The Sopranos* on DVD.

The due date approached, but there was nothing—no dilation, no Braxton-Hicks. The baby did not drop and so they waited, Sheila now sleeping on her side and struggling to get out of chairs. It was a gift of sorts. There was a little time to relax, and bank some sleep, not that it would make a difference, people said. It also allowed for a false sense of security. Matt began to feel ready. Things were organized and neat. There wasn't a sense that the baby was going to interfere with life as he had known it, because he was caught up and things were quiet. There was no unfinished business now, just Matt and Sheila and their unborn baby waiting to come out.

Matt went to work at the law firm and Sheila made it to her consulting job. She did something with benefits, though what exactly Matt could never say for sure. And why not go to work? There was no need to waste their limited maternity leave, no need to sit home and stew. And nothing happened; nothing until the call, that is.

"When are you getting home?" Sheila asked.

"I don't know," Matt said. "Six o'clock, maybe. I have some things to finish up here."

"Well, why don't you come home now? I feel...I don't know. I feel different today."

Matt went home immediately, but it wasn't like the movies, and he and Sheila were unsure when to leave for the hospital. It was impossible to figure out just how much time had elapsed between the contractions, or even what exactly a contraction was supposed to feel like. On top of that, Sheila's water never broke. When they finally went in to the hospital, the nurse said Sheila was not dilated enough, and needed to walk around for an hour before they would send her upstairs to give birth. They made it five minutes before Sheila couldn't walk at all.

The delivery room didn't seem much like the ones in the movies either. There were very few people present—just Sheila, Matt, the OB-GYN, and a nurse—and no one was running around yelling Stat!, which was calming, but disappointing in a way as well. A guy with hairy arms came by to do the epidural, but he didn't linger very long.

Sheila was asked to push, and then asked to push and breathe and push some more. Soon there was some hair that began to poke out with each push, only to disappear again when Sheila stopped. And then there was a head, a malformed head, though not as malformed as Matt first thought; the baby was just coming out facedown. And then there was a final push, and suddenly a baby, a perfect little boy with spiky hair, ten little fingers, and ten little toes.

And now there were five people in the room, though only one of them was screaming. And then when the doctor and nurse left the room only three—Matt, Sheila, and baby Charlie. Charlie was lovely, dark, lean and theirs. He wouldn't eat, though, or couldn't eat, it wasn't clear to them which; but that's okay, they thought. He's new; he'll figure it out. Anything was possible at this point, anything. There was a whole world out there for Charlie to learn about.

When he still wouldn't eat, though, they asked the nurse what she thought. "He just doesn't seem to be taking to my breast," Sheila said.

"Yes, and...?" the nurse said.

"Well, we're just not sure what to do."

"What do you think you should do?"

"I'm sorry. I don't understand."

"You're the parents," the nurse said. "It's up to you."

And yes, that was true—they had been parents for 24 hours now. But they didn't know anything, did they? Well, they must have, because the next day the hospital sent them home, just like that. "Unbelievable," Matt and Sheila said to each other at the time. "They just let you leave with one of these. How is that possible? How can they trust us to take care of this baby?" No one seemed to care, though, and no one seemed all that worried. "Amazing," they said again and again. "Fucking amazing."

They couldn't get the car seat fastened for the ride home. They had practiced this back in their house, but the straps weren't loosening up like they had on the couch. It was cold. They were tired. Charlie was wailing. Sheila held the car seat in place with her hands and prayed to any deity who might have been listening to spare them this one indiscretion.

They made it home safely, and quickly realized that they could make up all the rules they wanted concerning having a baby, but that they would still break them all by the end of the first week, if not the first day. Being good parents is great and all, Matt and Sheila thought, but the main goal is simple survival—both the baby's and yours.

And for the most part, they got by at first. They treated poor Charlie's diaper rash, tended to poor Charlie's circumcised penis, and swabbed the alien matter left behind after poor Charlie's umbilical cord had been cut. They even got him to eat, just a little at first, and then with Charlie finding his way, a lot. He was ravenous and making up for lost time.

A week passed, and there was hope. And then suddenly there wasn't. Charlie started to scream, from the moment he woke in the morning to the moment he finally drifted off at night. While Charlie would sleep in the evening for several hours after endless cooing, singing and rocking, and even go back to bed for an hour or two after a feeding, he might not sleep for the other seventeen hours of the day, choosing instead (assuming there was a choice) to scream shrill, bird-like, inhuman wails. He would hold his breath until he turned purple. He would sweat and ball up his beautiful little fists. But he could not be consoled, would not be consoled.

Charlie's pediatrician, a warm and calming presence, was happy to speculate on what might be going on. "Could be acid reflux," she said. It wasn't. "Maybe a lactose intolerance, then." No. "It's possible that he just wasn't ready to come out." Whatever that meant. "It's colic," she finally said. "We don't know what causes it, though it may be due to an immature digestive system. It will pass."

"Is there anything we can do?" Matt and Sheila said.

"Consider letting him sleep on his stomach. It may cause him less duress."

But they could not bring themselves to let Charlie sleep on his stomach, because of all the reports they had seen on television concerning SIDS, and because they could not do so they tried everything else. The bouncy seat. The vacuum cleaner. The swing with the uterine swoosh. But nothing worked, and the screaming continued, unabated.

One late night, as Charlie lay there on the ottoman in front of Matt, post-bottle, the screams since renewed for more than an hour,

Matt stared at him through his blurred vision and stinging eyes and suddenly found himself with the urge to pick Charlie up by his little baby shoulders and shake him as one might an adult, beseeching him to just tell Matt what he needed. We will do anything for you, Matt yelled inside his head. Anything. Matt had not moved an inch towards Charlie, but pulled himself away from the still-screaming baby anyway, wondering all the while what had become of him, what had become of them. Is this what Sheila and he had signed up for? Hadn't they been happy before this? Matt questioned if this was truly meant to be, or whether he had merely convinced himself that fatherhood was something he had wanted. He hated Charlie, he hated Sheila and he hated himself most of all.

Matt decided to lay little Charlie down on his belly. He needed some relief, and what else was there to do? He had not wanted to wake Sheila when Charlie had started screaming, which was probably a mistake, and wondered whether he should do so now before making this decision. He decided not to. He felt alone and locked into this path. It was his decision to make, and his alone. He lay Charlie face down in his bassinet. He wriggled for a moment, moving his face from side to side, looking for the right spot. And then he stopped. Stopped moving, stopped screaming, just stopped. His back began to rise and fall with his each breath, and he slept. No muss. No struggle. No furrowed brow.

Every five minutes for the next hour, Matt checked to make sure Charlie was still breathing; and then once he accepted that he was, wondered if he would continue to do so for the next five minutes. Matt was relieved, but anxious, and in the deepest recess of his brain wondered if maybe, just maybe, he had embraced the doctor's recommendation because of the small chance that Charlie might not make it through the night. This was possible, wasn't it? Of course it was. Matt also presumed, at least in part, that this was why he had not woken Sheila when he put Charlie down. He didn't want her to talk him out of it, nor did he want her to share in the burden of the decision. Matt wanted to think about all this further; but sleep overtook him, and he soon found himself unconscious on the floor next to the crib. He awoke around two hours later to Charlie's screams, as he had each day prior to this. Charlie had not died in his sleep and Matt was happy for that, but the screams had not gone away, and Matt had no idea how much longer this could possibly continue. They changed and fed him, but it didn't stop him from screaming, and there was of course nothing they could do about it. They decided to take him for a walk; they recognized that this would not likely bring Charlie any respite, but at least the screaming wouldn't sound so loud outside.

They headed down Pennsylvania Avenue, past the old Giant supermarket that had stood empty for years now, and the '80s tanning salon that no one ever went to anymore. They rolled by Bill's (the muffler place) that had once been Pudgies (the pizza parlor), where they could get two slices and a Coke for only 99 cents when they were kids, and the Hess station that never ran out of frozen burritos or wild-eyed clerks. They headed onto the off-ramp that took them towards downtown. It was crisp outside, with a slight breeze and the smell of burning leaves in the air, though no one appeared to be burning anything.

They hadn't been out much, something they hadn't realized until they actually left the house. It was easier to stay inside, isolated and alone, hiding from a world that couldn't help them and didn't want to deal with them. No one could possibly understand what they were going through. It was Matt and Sheila against the world, and there was no escape. Charlie was their problem—their problem to fix or die trying.

Being outside felt different, though. They felt lighter and freer out there, hopeful even. There were no walls closing them in, just a world of possibilities, and for a couple of minutes they really let themselves believe this. Charlie, however, wasn't feeling lighter or freer, though he could not articulate the reasons why in any particular way they could follow. There were no words for it because Charlie of course had no words. All he could do was cry and scream, tortured by a world he did not yet understand, but which he already knew had little to offer him in terms of comfort.

Charlie began to turn purple from all the crying, and while Matt and Sheila felt overwhelmed by some combination of anger, empathy, and powerlessness, there was nothing they could do but continue to walk along the overpass in silence, passing the old carwash and the closed bridge. Shortly they came upon the Park Diner, and decide to stop in. There may be no escape for them, from Charlie's endless distress, they thought, but at least they could have a cup of coffee and Charlie could be free from the restraints of his stroller.

After they ordered, Matt got up to use the bathroom, and as he passed the front entrance he began to feel shaky. Pausing for a moment, he closed his eyes, and little blips of light went off in his head. He looked back across the restaurant at Sheila, as she pulled Jones from the stroller to soothe him. She looked harried and tired.

We are in hell, Matt said to himself.

Matt wondered what it would be like to walk out the door and just keep walking, not stopping until he had reached some other city where he could start over, liberated and re-vitalized and with a new identity and a new life. Then he wondered why he was being so dramatic about it. Couldn't he just leave Sheila and Charlie and move to the other side of town? He could still support them, but why did he have to stay? People left their families all the time, didn't they? Why wasn't it okay for him to say he couldn't hack it, that he had to move on? Matt wasn't sure how to answer these questions; but then he looked back at Sheila again, holding Charlie, loving him, doing anything she could to bring him comfort, and he knew that it didn't matter. None of it mattered. They were in this together, and it was going to be all right. It had to be.

Matt walked back over to Sheila and Charlie. "I'm so fucking tired," he said.

"I know," Sheila said. "But we should go. Charlie is getting agitated."

"Sure. Let's get out of here."

And then suddenly, one day the screaming stopped just as randomly as it had started. Granted, Charlie would never end up being much for sleeping, no matter how old he eventually got, and would always remain a little obstinate as well; but in general he would turn out to be a pretty great kid, and a pretty great grown-up too. A couple of years later Matt and Sheila would also go on to have a daughter named Molly, who was nothing like Charlie had been. No screaming. No fussing. They would jokingly refer to her as "The Perfect Baby," the object of jealous parents at every fidgety school play and spring concert. And sometimes, Matt would think back on the days when Charlie was a baby, think about those days when the crying wouldn't stop. It seemed now sometimes like it had happened to a completely different person. And who knows; maybe it had.

Shooting Stick

HIS ONCE GRACEFUL FINGERS stroke his stubbly chin. He could have been a surgeon, people say; he could do anything with those fingers. But he hasn't, not besides shooting stick and wrapping them around a bottle of liquor, anyway. He looks off into the distance, at what I don't know. Does he? I doubt it; then again, I never knew what he was thinking, and I still don't. He never cared for me or taught me anything. He never gave me a home or a hug. He never came to one of my little-league games or took me to see a car show. He never helped me earn a merit badge or study long division. He never told me about sex or gave me any advice. He didn't read me bedtime stories or come to my room when I was scared late at night. He never said I love you or made the hurt go away. I guess when he decided it was all right to leave us that first time, something died in him. When I see old pictures of my father and my mother, when they were young and in love and before I came into the world, I see a glimmer of light dancing in his eyes, a glimmer that speaks volumes about love and dreams and hope. Now those very same eyes are dull and lifeless, prone to staring off into space, no longer searching for that thing that is now long lost.

I used to wait for my dad to visit. I'd sit there by the window late at night, searching for him like a cop's wife must do. Every shadow might be him, I thought; but no, it never was. "He's off on a business trip," my mom would say. "He'll be home soon." But I knew better. I knew that he was a spy, like James Bond, traveling the world on secret missions, saving us from evil, slowing down just long enough to have drinks and gamble with some babe with a name like Pussy Galore. Or perhaps he was a cowboy off on some ranch somewhere; or maybe an astronaut just a few weeks away from his ticker-tape parade. I would search at night, looking for his spaceship, and with every shooting star I'd think, That's my old man, right there, on his way home.

Once I was older, I'd spy him downtown every so often, usually in the window of some bar, and once in awhile he would come by the house to visit, always wearing a suit but the suit always rumpled and dirty, him always thinner, withering away layer by layer, his looks and youth fading like an old coat of paint. When he came to visit he would ask for a little pocket change, just something to tide him over, and I would run to get my piggybank, only too eager to help out.

"This is the last time I do this, Petey boy, I swear," he'd say to me. "Now mind your mom and do your schoolwork."

"Sure, dad," I'd say, giving him a little wave as he made his way to the bus stop.

One time when he came by he asked if I wanted to shoot some pool with him. He said he had a couple of extra dollars, and what did I think? "Yes, yes, absolutely," I said, a little too quickly. We went down to the arcade by the high school. It was real smoky, the windows covered with dark stick-on shades, and there were games everywhere—Centipede and Pole Position, Asteroids and Pac-Man. Lights were flashing and bells were ringing, and the room was filled with surly, long-haired teenagers, sporting wispy mustaches and wearing soiled three-quarter-length jerseys emblazoned with logos of metal bands. I felt like we had invaded some sort of hidden teenage sanctum, and it was all a bit scary to me, actually. In fact, I would have been just as happy to leave, but I certainly wasn't going to say anything to my dad. Meanwhile, he seemed right at home there, and I knew there was no turning back when he placed two quarters on the railing of the pool table.

We stood there until the game being played was over, me still fidgety and nervous, my dad still completely relaxed. The winners looked over at us and my dad walked over to the table, inserting our quarters and racking the balls. I missed every shot, needless to say; but the thing is that my dad was just awesome. He was using English and adding all sorts of spins, hitting shots from every possible angle, and never talking, just cruising around the table silently pointing at pockets with the tip of his stick. Soon enough the game was over, and we had won, and just like that the table was suddenly under our control.

The next set of teenagers approached the table, and now they had to rack, and we got to break, and I still didn't hit a thing, but it didn't matter, because there was my dad once again walking around the table in that ratty old suit of his, stalking those balls, not missing a shot. He was a god out there, and just like that we won again. At this point the whole place is watching—and they had to, of course, I mean, who were we to come into their space and take over like that? And who was this guy running every shot with some loser kid as his partner? No one could answer those questions, and no one immediately emerged to play us for the table either. Instead the teenagers quietly conferred amongst themselves, and then decided to send their best two players forward to challenge us.

It was two girls, both wearing tight Jordache jeans and feathered hairdos, and they could really play. I mean, they weren't better than my dad, but then he was also carrying me. Soon they're matching my dad shot for shot, and the place is just totally silent, everyone watching, the four of us in our own little world. The tension mounts, and then there is just the eight-ball remaining, and the one girl misses it, leaving it just sitting there hanging on the lip of the pocket, just waiting for someone to tap it in. That someone is me, and it's a lot of green because she's also managed to leave the cue ball on the exact opposite end of the table. The girls start getting ready for their next shot, simply assuming I'm going to miss; it's a straight-enough shot, though, and my dad is coaching me. "Use the lights, Petey. Relax. Breathe. You can do it. You're cool as a cucumber." And so I line up the shot, and I close my eyes, and I strike the cue ball, and the eight-ball drops; and we are triumphant, and they are dejected, and we leave as the undefeated champions.

Unfortunately I started to see him less and less after that summer, and then he finally stopped coming by to visit at all. At first, the less I saw him, the more I dreamt about him. I'd open the door to my room and a skeleton in a cheap suit would be standing there, smiling, arms outstretched, looking for a hug. I'd burrow deeper and deeper into my covers until he went away, all the while crying silent tears because tough guys didn't cry. But even the dreams stopped coming at some point, and as I grew older I stopped waiting by the window, stopped staring into the sky and mistaking shooting stars for his ship. Finally, my dad became just another one of the shadows I conducted small talk with down at happy hour at Tom and Marty's on a Friday afternoon; and while we never had much to say to one another, he would always bring up the day of the pool game, the day his boy, all calm and cool and collected, had hit the shot that had beat the best players in the arcade.

Then he fell ill, or maybe he just fell, and now he spends most of his time staring out a window, and now it's me that sees his face brighten when he spies me coming up the front walk. The other day I took him down to the old arcade; it's dingy and uncared for now, empty of videogames because no one plays videogames at arcades anymore. The pool table is still there, though, and there's no one using it when we arrive, so we chalk up our cues and rack the balls.

We don't last very long, three games maybe, and the shooting is poor. "If you want to know the truth," I say laughing, "I feel kind of bad taking advantage of a chemo patient."

"A chemo patient who can still kick your ass," he says, laughing back. He gets a faraway look in his eyes when I line up my next shot. "Hey, remember the time you beat the girls?" he asks.

"Sure," I say, watching him lean forward just a little too much, watching him catch himself on the table's edge when he thinks no one is looking. "Luckiest shot I've ever made."

"That wasn't luck," he says. "You were master of the universe that day."

I laugh again. "Just shoot, asshole."

And then we're done almost as soon as we've started. And I take him home, and I help him up the stairs and into his apartment. And then I make sure he's comfortable and that he has a warm dinner that's ready to eat, before I leave him once again staring out the window. And as I walk away I realize that I have lied about something. I said that he never taught me anything, but that's not true. He taught me how easy it can be not to give a shit. And in this, he really has left me something I legitimately treasure.

So Different Now
2011

So Different Now

SHE'S RIGHT THERE IN THIRSTY'S. In her usual spot. Drinking her usual drink. Yuengling on tap. One after another.

And he's there too. Behind the bar. Pouring drinks. One after another.

Sometimes they speak. But mostly she orders. He pours. And so it goes.

The three of us, Becky, Jamie and me, went to MacArthur elementary school together. MacArthur was built on top of a swamp and now allegedly sinks one millimeter into the ground every year, year in and year out. Of course, maybe that's just the local folklore.

Becky had lived over by St. Johns Church, near Mill Hill. Her older brother Billy was a famous high school drunk. Her dad had died when we were all young—it was something on a construction site—and her mom always looked harried. Becky took care of herself from the start. She got herself up for school. Got dinner made and even paid the bills when needed.

She also followed me around. At first it was just around school, moving desks to be closer to me, maybe changing tables in the lunchroom. It was harmless. But then I started seeing her as I was leaving school. Drifting across the lawn, watching me, following me with her eyes and then everyday venturing just that much further, up the hill in front of school and towards the crosswalk and the crossing guard, the one who had lost her nose to cancer and now wore this triangle thing in the spot where her nose had been.

And then she moved past the crosswalk and the creepy house where the old shut-in lady lived, the one who waved to me as I walked to and from school even as she plotted to lure me into her home so she could bake me into some kind of stew or possibly touch my dick. Soon enough Becky was past the shut-in's house and Dave Jordan's house as well, Dave whose step-dad never spoke much after coming home from Vietnam and never could stand for any kind of noise in the yard.

I kept looking over my shoulder, but Becky was there, coming, coming after me, up the street and towards my house, and I am running now, the sweat trickling down my back as I head up the hill in front of my house and through the front door, where I am safe and can play Missile Command before I go out to see my friends because she is gone.

Except that she isn't.

"Who's the girl sitting on the front lawn?" my dad Jones asks, walking in. "She's cute." My dad isn't living with us right now, but he's home to make dinner, because everything is going to be like it always is.

"Becky is on the front lawn?" I say.

"Becky? Sure. Should we invite her in?"

"No, no, what am I going to do?"

"Do, do about what?"

"Leaving the house!"

My dad pauses. He knows something about leaving the house.

"Here's what you do," he says. "You put on your Lone Ranger mask and just leave, walk right by her, no eye contact, no looking back."

"Yeah?"

"Yeah. It'll work like a charm."

And so I do, never looking back and never really talking to her again.

"Hey, Becky," I say back at Thirsty's. "Can I get you a drink?"

"Are you sure?"

"Yeah, why?"

I know why. She knows why. We haven't talked in twenty-five years. Still, she looks good, decent. She has nice eyes, kind eyes. Plus, the fact is my wife Marsha is fucking our friend Tommie and I am the last to find out.

"I'll have a Yuengling," she says.

"Cool."

"Jamie," she yells, motioning Jamie over. "Another Yuengling."

"Two," I shout.

"Sure," he grunts.

Jamie walks over to the tap.

"Are you friends with him?" I ask Becky.

"Why?" she says cautiously.

"I don't know," I say. "He seems kind of weird with that bad bowl haircut and those fucked-up teeth. Well, and that shit back in high school."

Jamie had terrorized us when we were kids. He was bigger than we were. And mean. Smashing our ears on the bus with the palms of his hands and messing with our bikes if we left them unattended for even a second; endlessly pelting us with rocks, ice balls and crabapples; grabbing our nipples, or worse, our balls in the locker room after swim class, grabbing them hard, and then pausing, his smile malicious and hungry.

We knew enough to know that his home life was fucked up, all poor and violent, but we didn't care, he was a fucking bully, and we all hated him, suppressing our anger and fear, because we couldn't fight him and there was no one to tell. No one's parents were ever around, and even if they had been, who was going to talk to Jamie's fat fucking father Joey? No one; no one's dad was that tough or scary.

And then he was gone, as if abducted by aliens, which we would have believed and enjoyed. But no, the rumor was that he had been sent to a home for juvenile delinquents. For what we didn't know, but did it matter? No. We were free, until we weren't. In high school the rumors started up again. Jamie was coming back. He had done his time. We all started getting tense and worked-up. If Jamie had been a bully before they sent him away, what would he be like now?

He wasn't a bully. He wasn't even tough. He was small now, smaller than all of us, like he had stopped growing. And maybe he had. He was also soft. His shoulders perpetually bowed. Quiet, dressed in his Anderson-Little oxfords, he never spoke, never really looked up from the ground. He was scared of everything, you could smell it. Rumors were that he had been raped wherever it was they sent him, which seemed possible, because here he was, fucked up and different.

"I don't think any of that stuff people said about him was true," Becky says.

"No?" I reply.

"No. He had a rough time, but he's better now."

"Yeah? How do you know?" I ask, looking right at her.

"Can we talk about something else?"

"Sure. How about I walk you home?"

"Yeah, okay, why not."

We walk down Vestal Avenue towards Becky's house, past

Robby's Liquor Store and the old post office. We walk into her house and we are both quiet, anticipating something that already seems likely to happen.

"Do you want a beer?" Becky asks me.

"Okay."

"So, your wife is banging Tommy," she says matter-of-factly.

"That's what I hear."

"Is that why you're here?"

"Can we talk about something else?"

"Yeah, okay. What?"

"You know what? Maybe we could just fuck."

"Okay, sure."

And so we do.

The next day I am at work and I am thinking about Becky and how it's even possible that I'm doing so all these years later. She told me that she's off work today, though it's not remotely clear to me that she actually does anything besides drink at Thirsty's. I walk over to Robby's during lunch, grab a six-pack of Yuengling and decide to surprise her.

As I get to her house I see Jamie sitting on her porch. He's dragging a knife back and forth along the table in front of him. He looks up at me. He's glaring.

"Hey," I say. "Is Becky home?"

"She's my fucking girlfriend," he says quietly, still dragging the knife, still looking at me.

"What?"

"You heard me," he shouts. "Becky is my fucking girlfriend, my girlfriend, my fucking *girlfriend.*"

My heart starts to pound. "I-I-I didn't know," I stammer.

"My fucking girlfriend," he says, slamming the knife into the table and walking away.

I knock on Becky's door. She opens it. She's been crying. I don't feel bad, just furious, though why I do is hard to say.

"What the fuck," I say. "Jamie's your boyfriend?"

"Yeah," she says, looking beaten down.

"What the fuck?"

She doesn't say anything.

"Why didn't you say something?"

Nothing.

"What the fuck?"

"You were making fun of him," she says, starting to cry again.

"What are you, fucking five years old?"

Nothing, more crying.

"Seriously, why didn't you say something?"

"Because it was you," she says.

In a Single Bound

"SO," SHE SAYS, SMILING. "Do you think this guy is stalking you or what?"

They are going out to lunch together. She is Molly the intern. She is young and vibrant, if a little weird and awkward, with her interest in graphic novels, Spider-Man, and him, all things he is interested in as well.

He normally makes it a point to avoid the younger employees, especially the female ones. He wants to get to work, get what needs to be done, done, and then get home to his wife, and his real life. Because that's the thing; like Spider-Man he lives in two worlds, and his real life has little to do with work or who he is at work. Spider-Man is both a superhero and an everyman struggling to pay his bills and deal with a boss who doesn't appreciate his job performance. And that's him as well, just in reverse. He is a superhero at work, but the rest of the time he is just a regular guy trying to deal with people's expectations of him, his wife included.

It's not that his wife doesn't appreciate him. It's just that his wife doesn't appreciate him like Molly the intern does. Molly the intern has no expectations at all, and frankly it's refreshing. The risk in this kind of relationship, though, is in the inherent power differential between Molly the intern and him, a mix of age and status and gender; and superhero or not, he doesn't always know how to manage that. The boundaries aren't always clear.

Even worse, there are his fears about opportunity, or perceived opportunity. He doesn't want to be distracted by some other woman while at work or at home when he is with his wife, the wife who he loves. He doesn't want to be forced to ask what if? What if she wants him? What if he could fuck her? What if he found himself in a position he could not get out of? Because here's the thing—it is Molly the intern that allows him to see himself as a superhero at work. She treats him as someone worthy of worship and admiration, and every superhero knows this can be a trap.

Just the other day, for example, he was in his office when he noticed one of the other Directors corner Molly the intern out in the hall. "Do you want to hear a story?" he said to her.

"Sure," she said, not knowing if she was even allowed to say no.

"I was at this biker rally over the weekend and this scary motorcycle dude and his even scarier girlfriend walked up to me and he says, 'Hey man, do you want to see my cock?'"

Molly the intern smiled nervously. She did not want to be part of this, but she didn't know how to get out of it either. He wondered if he needed to do something, but waited to see what would unfold.

"Anyway," the Director said, leaning in closer to the intern. "I must have looked at him weirdly, because then scary motorcycle guy said to me, 'You're sick, dude, I meant my tattoo' and then he rolled up his sleeve and showed me this tattoo he had of a rooster. That's funny, right?"

Again Molly the intern smiled nervously and he realized it was now time to take action.

"And that wasn't even the end of it," the Director continued, "because then the guy's girlfriend looked at me and said, 'How about I show you my pussy…'"

"Hey," he said, swooping in and putting his arm around the Director's shoulder, steering him away from Molly the intern. "There's this thing you can help me with. Come take a look."

"I'm telling a story…"

"It can wait," he said, hustling the Director into his office.

When he looked back, Molly the intern mouthed "thank you" and he knew her appreciation was real and true, though unnecessary, since he had only done what any concerned citizen would do.

Still, not everyone is inclined to do the right thing; and while the superhero may have no choice in the matter, any superhero worth his salt knows that their reasons for doing the right thing can be complicated by feelings other than valor. But then, Molly the intern is different. She may be vibrant and interesting, but he's not attracted to her and it is liberating. He can be himself and he can talk about things like whether Spider-Man broke Gwen Stacy's neck that horrible day on the George Washington Bridge or if in fact the Green Goblin had already done so. She cares about this stuff and his wife doesn't. And maybe it's not all that important, really, but it is to him and it reminds him of what he once was and what has been lost.

He wonders sometimes whether he can ever be that guy again. The guy he was before he got married to a woman he loved, and let go of all those things that defined him before they met and decided to embark on a life together. He doesn't know the answer to this, and he certainly doesn't know how someone would go back, even if they decided it was the most important thing in the world to them. Instead he is here alone with Molly the intern at the Park Diner for lunch because she suggested that they get away from the office and all the distractions there. They are sitting in the back dining room, the one with the painting of Icarus who is forever falling and the big windows that overlook the river and its endlessly tricky eddies and whirlpools.

"So," she says, smiling. "Do you think this guy is stalking you or what?"

It's funny, her labeling the guy from accounting a stalker, like the guy is the supervillain in this story. He doesn't even really know the guy from accounting, but that doesn't matter to Molly the intern, because superheroes need archenemies if they are going to be superheroes, and she knows this as surely as she knows anything. This makes him think about his wife. His wife is no villain, mind you, but she is an essential part of the story. He is dependent on her, at least the idea of her and what she represents—home, safety, stability. Even superheroes need to escape to their other lives once in a while and she is that life.

Still, it's an odd thing really to feel so intensely self-righteous about what it means to look at other women and even fantasize about them. He knows how much he doesn't want to do this and how wrong it feels, because he also knows that if you bend anything too much, even relationships, they will break; and that even if they can be repaired, they are never quite the same. Betrayal is tricky like that, because betraying someone you love is like killing them in some ways. And once it's done, it's done, and you can't ever escape the realization that what you did was wrong, even if you didn't intend to do it. It doesn't work like that.

But again, it's different with Molly the intern. She knows that Spider-Man didn't intend for his Uncle Ben to be murdered, and that he certainly didn't consciously intend to betray him. Spider-Man was caught up in something new and exciting, and it was a mistake that he would have done anything to fix once he realized what had happened. And that's the thing with her; she knows that this distinction is important, because it makes Spider-Man human and flawed and worthy of empathy, something his wife does not understand and never has.

So, does it help that he truly has no feelings for Molly the intern and that she has none for him? That they can stay up late drinking at the office Christmas party and he can tell her how marriages get stale? And that no, she shouldn't marry young because there is so much to see and do and he should know. That he might even have done it differently and that he might still do it differently if given the chance.

Of course it does.

"So," she says, smiling. "Do you think this guy is stalking you or what?"

"What do you mean?" he says.

"You know, the guy from accounting," she says. "You were saying how you'll suddenly notice him sitting next to you in meetings, and how he just happens to be in places like the post office or Thirsty's. Like he somehow knows where you'll be, like it's a coincidence."

"Did I say that?" he asks, because he doesn't really remember doing so. "That's funny."

"What's funny?" she says.

"For one, that you think I said that," he says. "But also because for a moment you sounded like you were describing yourself."

She recoils. Settles herself into her chair. Forces a smile. "Why would you say that?" she says. "That's so fucked up."

"I didn't mean anything by it," he says, and he didn't. Did he? "It's just that sometimes you suddenly pop up next to me at meetings or at Thirsty's. And it reminds me of that story you told me that time about that guy you were in that class with who thought you were stalk...following him around."

He stops talking. He realizes how selfish he has been. How it's all been about some vague fantasy for him, but it hasn't been for her. For Molly the intern, all this has been real, and because it has, he has not only betrayed his wife, he has betrayed her as well. The terrible thing is that he didn't see this coming. He was blind to what was happening. And now here he is, in an empty room with her, a room that he came to willingly, even as the trap was being set, and even as he should have known better.

A good supervillain, he thinks, always recognizes the superhero's vulnerabilities better than the superhero does; and in knowing this the villain is able to capitalize on them before the superhero can do anything about it. The superhero always escapes, though, just as Spider-Man does time and time again. That's just how it works. The thing is, sometimes—most of the time—the superhero's escape involves the use of force and the villain is hurt, or even killed, just as the Green Goblin was. In this sense, he now realizes, the superhero is also a supervillain, because a villain cannot exist without a hero making them what they are; and yet to remain a superhero, the superhero must ultimately destroy them. There is no other way.

"I don't follow you," she says again, forcing a smile.

"I think you do," he says. "And I'm really sorry, but I should go and we need to stop doing this."

She wants to be composed, cool, but little cracks are starting to appear. "'This,'" she says. "I don't know what 'this' is. I don't know what you're talking about."

"I'm sorry," he says, trying to sound firm.

Molly The intern suddenly gets up and closes the door to the room they are in, a door he never even noticed until now. "You're sorry," she says, leaning against the door and standing between him and freedom. "This isn't right. You don't just get to pull back like that."

"Let me get the check," he says, starting to panic. "I'm done talking about this."

"You asshole," she says. "Did you really believe that I gave a shit about Spider-Man?"

Did he really believe it? Maybe. But did he really want to believe it? More than anything.

Stevey

STEVEY BRANCUSI WAS THE COOLEST. He had the biggest smile. The best hair. The slickest dad. And the chicks loved Stevey, fucking loved him. We of course idolized Stevey; we had to. We had nowhere else to turn.

"You never, ever, take a dump at a girl's house," Stevey would say. "It might smell, or you could fart and then you're really fucked."

"Can you take a piss?" we would ask.

"If you have to, but flush while you piss. You don't want any extra noise, nothing, got it?"

"Got it."

We accepted Stevey's advice because Stevey got laid; and because we didn't yet know the difference between being confident and being smart, it was all one in the same to us.

Stevey also dated Stacey Bloom, the hottest girl any of us had ever seen. She was ravishing, like a fire gone crazy with her tremendous mane of red hair, all long and feathered, and framing her freckled face and high cheekbones. Stacey's breasts were perfect as well, round and full and endlessly straining the buttons of the little girlie oxfords everyone was wearing then. We bowed at Stacey's feet, and we were happy to. She ran the school with that hair and those breasts, and the fact that Stevey had access to both of them only further ensured our rapt attention to anything and everything he had to say.

It wasn't that Stevey didn't have quirks though. He didn't like dirt, for example, and more specifically he didn't like dirty fingernails.

"Trim your nails," Stevey would say. "They have to look neat and clean at all times."

"All right, Stevey," we would say.

"And don't ever date girls with dirty nails," he would say. "If they don't have clean nails, then you know they can't be all that clean in general. Just the other day Holly Bingham invited me over to her place and offered to blow me. I thought about it, but then I saw her nails. They were fucking disgusting, all chewed-up and dirty. Fuck that, I told her."

"Not even for a blowjob?" we said.

"Not even. I wouldn't even let her blow you guys with those nails."

It made sense, all of it, because in a world with little guidance, Stevey was willing to provide some. We didn't always believe him, but we didn't care; we needed him. We were out of control, crazy for girls and careening from one fuck-up to the next. Stevey was in control, though, and we loved that.

The night after the basketball team wins the state quarterfinals we all go to a party at Arnold Long's house, one of the rare occasions when jocks and cheerleaders mix with the rest of us. It's rocking—babes, alcohol, everyone hooking up left and right. I'm approached by Frankie Hill, a cheerleader and a senior. She has long wavy blonde hair, a little pug nose and dirty jeans. She's from the east side of town and a little trashy.

"Hey," Frankie says. "You're friends with Stevey Brancusi, right?"

"Yeah, yeah, I am," I say.

"Cool, he's real cute," she says.

"Yes he is," I say. "I could introduce you to him sometime if you want."

"No, that's all right, we've met," she says.

"Okay," I say. "So you want to get another beer or something?"

"No, let's go upstairs," Frankie says.

And so we do. Soon I'm on top of her, kissing and thrusting, and she's kissing me back. And then she's thrusting too, and moaning, and wrapping her legs around me. I'm enjoying myself, but I'm worried as well. What if she wants to have sex? How will I know? Do I just ask? I start to fumble with her zipper and she seems cool with that. Do I reach for a condom now? And how long has the condom been in my wallet anyway? Will she give me some sort of sign if she wants to go further? I make contact with her panties. Should I wait to say something? And if so, how long should I wait? I start to panic.

"So, uhh, do you want have sex?" I blurt out.

She stops thrusting, and moaning, and kissing. "Are you kidding me?" she says. I look down at her and there is this moment where I wonder what it would be like to hold her down. I don't do it—I don't even come close to doing it—but I see in her eyes that she knows I was thinking about it. She looks scared for a moment, and then realizing nothing is going to happen, she rolls away. I never see her again.

"You shouldn't have asked her if she wanted to have sex," Stevey says. "You've got to be cool. You never rush them. If you have to ask because you don't know the answer, it's not the right time. Patience, man, patience. You could've nailed her the next time you got together."

And of course he was right, or maybe he wasn't, but it didn't matter. We didn't have older brothers who could tell us what they knew, and our dads were never around. Maybe they had moved out or moved on, maybe they were working, or maybe they just wouldn't talk to us. But Stevey was around, and so was his dad Richie, and they were willing to help.

Richie had been a star athlete in his day, and still exuded a cool that none of us had ever seen before. He would come by soccer practice on his motorcycle, walk over to us and gather us up in a little group, a toothpick protruding from the side of his mouth, his "Kiss Me I'm Italian" cap cocked to the side just so, and he would look at us with his big welcoming smile and just start giving us advice.

"Boys, no one can concentrate on more than two things at once, not if they want to do them well. You boys have to study, and you have to come to practice, and if you hope to do well in these endeavors then you don't have time for anything else."

"What about girls?" we'd say.

"What about girls," he'd say, a little smile crossing his face. "You definitely don't have time for them."

And we accepted that, but we just didn't listen. We couldn't listen.

One night we're over at Stevey's house, sitting around his kitchen table and talking about fighting.

"Fighting is for pussies," Stevey says.

"Why?" we say.

"Because it's a sign of weakness, and you never want to look weak," Stevey says. "You think weak guys get laid?"

"No?" we say with hesitation.

"Damn straight. That said," Stevey says, "if you have to fight, get real close to the guy, get in the first punch and make it count. Most guys will back down after that."

As we contemplate this, we hear Richie's motorcycle pull up in the driveway. It's late and he's just getting home from work.

"Hey boys," Richie says as he walks into the kitchen.

"Hi Mr. Brancusi," we say.

"Where have you been, pops?" Stevey says.

"I had to give the dispatch girl a ride home," Richie says. "Her car broke down."

"You gave her a ride home on your motorcycle?" Stevey says.

"Yeah," Richie says with his big smile. "And you should have seen her, boys. She pressed right up against me with her thighs on my hips and that long hair flying, working with me on every turn, knowing when to shift her weight. She really knew what she was doing. A real pro, that one. It was incredible, fucking incredible, nothing like your mom, Stevey boy, I'll tell you that."

A rare grimace crosses Stevey's face, and then a momentary look of anger, but it's brief, and soon he's smiling again. We never saw Stevey's mother much. She was always in the house, but she tended to sit back and live in the shadows, furtively moving from room to room, like a cat burglar in her own home. Sometimes you would get a look at her, but she was always wearing these big sunglasses and so you never really could make eye contact with her or anything like that.

"Hey," Stevey says. "Who wants to go to State Park? Stacey and her friends have rented a cabin up there and said we should stop by. Who knows, maybe one of you numbnuts will even get laid."

We don't need any more convincing than that. We all pile into Stevey's car and head out to the park.

"You guys are all wearing anti-perspirant, right?" Stevey says.

"Yeah," we all say.

"Good. You don't need deodorant—I mean, do any of you actually smell?" he says.

"No," we say.

"Of course not. But anti-perspirant is different," he says. "You never want chicks to see you sweat. Never. Sweat is the biggest fucking turn-off you can imagine."

"Worse than taking a dump in their house?" we say laughing.

"Yeah," Stevey says, "I guess...hey, fuck you. I'm trying to help you here."

"What about dirty nails? Is sweat worse than dirty nails?" we say, laughing some more.

"Hey, seriously, fuck you guys," Stevey says. "I've been trying to help you losers. Fuck it, just fuck it."

No one says a word the rest of the ride. We had thought we were joking around, but somewhere we have crossed a line and no one knows exactly what happened. Maybe we saw that Stevey was a little more vulnerable than usual after the exchange with Richie, and maybe we had pushed him a little too hard. Maybe we found ourselves resenting the fact that he wasn't in control all the time, that he was flawed, and that we hated ourselves for trusting him so much when he struggled just like everyone else did.

When we get to the cabin, girls are everywhere, drunk and staggering around. They've been drinking all day and Stacey is so wasted she can barely walk, as Stevey drags her away from the group and off into the woods near the cabin.

I idle around the keg for awhile, trying to make small talk, and hoping I don't look like the idiot I know myself to be. As I stand there, I notice Jessica Bloom, Stacey's younger sister sitting off by herself on one of the picnic tables. Jessica is certainly not as hot as Stacey, nor does she possess Stacey's sense of cool, but she has beautiful skin, lips so full they're almost ripe, and an adorable little nose. She seems vulnerable, and sensitive, and you want to hug her when you see her, but you never would.

Tonight she's wearing this big down coat, hugging her knees to her chest, and rocking back and forth. I don't know if I should disturb her, but she once smiled at me in the hall at school. I want her, and if there's any chance anything could ever happen I'm going to need to talk to her at some point.

"Hey…hey Jessica," I say. "Can I get you a beer?"

No response.

"Jessica," I say a little louder. "How's it going?"

She looks over at me as if waking from a dream. "Oh hey," she says. "I didn't know anyone was there. How are you?" She looks sad; it could be the alcohol, but there's something more there, I just don't know what.

"I'm fine," I say. "How are you? Is everything all right?"

"Yeah," she says. "I'm fine, really. Just cold."

I know she's lying to me, and though Stevey has never said anything about it, I know that guys who know how to show some compassion can get over.

"Are you sure you're okay?" I say. "Do you want to talk?"

Jessica pauses, and then she says, "All right. Can I trust you? I mean really trust you? Because you can't go off and repeat this."

"Yeah, of course," I say. "What is it?"

Jessica's lips, her wonderful lips, quiver for a moment, and tears begin to well up in her eyes. "So, are you good friends with Stevey?" she says.

"Pretty good friends, I guess. Why, what's that got to do with anything?"

"Well, you know he and Stacey are a couple, right?"

"Yeah," I say. "Of course."

Jessica has stopped looking at me at this point. She's just talking and staring off into the night.

"He hits her," she says suddenly. "He hits her, my beautiful sister, and she won't do anything about it."

I had heard of things like this before in the movies, but I never thought they really happened. And Stevey hitting Stacey, it makes no sense. She's a fucking goddess.

"What," I say. "C'mon, really?"

"Yeah," she says. "And she won't leave him, and she won't listen to me, and I don't know what to do anymore."

At this point Jessica starts to sob uncontrollably, and I anxiously and awkwardly put my arm around her shoulders. She lowers her head onto my chest and it's nice. Peaceful. I feel sick, though, and angry, but I don't know what to say, so we just sit there, shivering, not talking, just breathing, sad and lost.

Moments later, Stevey and Stacey emerge from the woods, smiling and laughing. Stacey is stumbling and Stevey is holding her up.

"Look at this," Stevey says. "Look at the lovebirds. I guess my advice isn't so bad, is it?"

I walk over to Stevey. I stand right in front of him and I punch him in the face as hard as I can, just like he taught me to.

Cool, Not Removed

J. MY THERAPIST is what you might expect. Tweed jackets, year-round; sweater vests; corduroys; and a thatch of brown, parted, college-professor hair.

J.'s office is in a nondescript building downtown by the old Ramada Inn. The halls are long, windowless, and generally empty. The waiting room is normal enough. A few chairs, a clock radio always tuned to NPR, and the usual mix of magazines strewn about the room—*Rolling Stone, O, People.* When I arrive I press a button next to J.'s name, a light goes on, and this means he has been notified of my presence.

When J. comes to get me, I pass through a door, cross another hall—more narrow this time—and then enter the office itself. J.'s office also looks like what you might expect. There are two big chairs; piles of random files, loose-leaf paper jutting out at various angles; a seldom-used computer; and an endless array of books—Kafka, Faulkner, Dickens—stacked on shelves from floor to ceiling.

"So, how are you doing?" J. asks.

"Fine, good, all right," I say. "I've been thinking about this married friend of mine. Happy. Married to his college sweetheart. Two kids, one on the way. Little ranch house. Big backyard. They have friends. And he's not like other guys I know who are ten years into their marriage and fucking their buddy's wife in the backseat of some car during their lunch breaks. Sure, he looks around. A lot. The women are only getting younger. It's nice. They're fresh, their skin like that of a freshly picked peach. But it's just looking. Nothing more. Well, he once gave a foot rub to one of the moms in his wife's playgroup while she sat there pregnant and topless, but that was on a dare. Otherwise, no misbehaving, none, not this friend, he wouldn't do it.

"Still, he went to his high-school reunion recently. Solo. The wife didn't want to go. He understood. She doesn't know these people. Doesn't care about them. Plus, someone's got to watch the kids, and getting a babysitter is such a hassle, and he gets all that too. He even secretly celebrates it. No wife for the night, it's liberating, like getting a 'get out of jail free' card. Now, does he feel like being married is like being in jail? No, of course not, not for the most part anyway. There are moments, though. Does he get to do whatever he wants whenever he wants? No, not at all. Does he care? Not really. But is that kind of like being in prison? Sure it is, a little.

"So, no wife, but there are a bunch of aging, pasty misanthropes there he once knew, once drank with, now living largely sedate lives, doing things like him. Are there sparks at times? Likely, but overall not so much. All seem fine, mostly satisfied, keeping on, keeping on. And so it goes. He wanders around Thirsty's, the location of the Friday night icebreaker, shows off pictures of his kids, drinks a little too much, and then hunkers down at the bar to catch his breath and regain his balance.

"He rubs his eyes and when he looks up she's sitting there. It's been twenty years, but it's her. She still has long, light brown hair and a crooked little smile. She still has dancer's legs. And she's sitting right there. Where did she come from?

"'Hey man,' she says, smiling.

"He's floored. He has thought about her over the years, wondering where she might have gone and what might have happened to her. He had longed for her back in high school, madly, crazily, and it was somewhat mutual, but it was never the right time for them, and little came of it. One night they had sat on a stairwell at a party talking for hours, oblivious to the chaos going on around them, and by morning he was sure that he was in love with her. Another time she had come to his house when he was having a party and she had wanted to get together with him. He had a girlfriend then, and she was there as well, but they had kissed, finally. It was amazing, but he panicked, backed off, didn't want to get caught. He thought there would be more chances to get together, but there weren't, and he had never seen her again. And now here she was.

"'How are you,' he says. 'It's been so long. What have you been up to?'

"'What have I been up to?' she says. 'I don't know, this and that. Never married though, couldn't find the right guy. You?'

"'I'm married,' he says. 'Great wife, two kids, it's good. Real good. Yeah. It's wild seeing you, though. Fuck. Weird.'

"'Yeah,' she says. 'You seem happy, though. Why didn't I meet someone like you?'

"'I don't know,' he says, 'but you will.'

"'Maybe,' she says. 'How come we never got together?'

"'I don't know,' he says. 'Why do you think we never got together?'

"'I'm not sure,' she says, 'but I know you freaked out that one time. That could have been our shot. You ever wonder what might have been if we had gone for it that night? I know you're happy and all, but still, do you ever wonder? I do.'

"They talk for hours. He hasn't felt that way in years. Maybe ever, or at least not since the last they spoke like this on the stairwell. He can't decide if this is really happening, or even what this is. He knows it's fake, but does it have to be? Because he also knows he doesn't want it to end. Night becomes morning. He has to leave. She asks him to stay longer and go to breakfast with her to Park Diner at least, maybe? Why not? It's okay, she says, this isn't real. He knows this, but hearing her say it reminds him that the real world awaits him. He gets in his car. He drives away. He tries not to think about what might have been."

"Your time is just about up," J. says. "We will need to talk about this further during your next visit."

This is fine with me. You cover what you can during the forty-five minutes you have, and then you move on. Week to week, J. and I talk about the things that are going on in my life—work, family, and other stressors. We try to draw connections between events and look at ways to respond to problems, past, current, future. Sometimes I get kind of emotional and sometimes I do not. Either way, I leave when my time is up, and I re-enter the real world, and reality, no longer as supported or safe as I just was in the protective cocoon of the office, but now better able to re-experience life in all its messy chaos. I try to keep everything constant and balanced, not too high, not too low, always pushing, but cool, not removed, but still more tightly wrapped then I would like to be. And most of the time this works fine.

On this day then, the session ends as it always does, and while this may be unimportant, what happens next is not. When I leave the waiting room, the fire doors about halfway down the hall are closed. They've never been closed before, and I wonder why this is. I am struck by the feeling that the always empty halls have never seemed ominous before, but today they do. And that the typically straightforward sterility of the building my therapist's office is located in has never seemed imposing, but today it does. Even the call button in my therapist's office seems suspect at this moment and this time. What is my therapist hiding from? Who is he trying to keep out?

I stand in front of the fire doors, wondering if they are locked, and the idea of opening them makes me uncomfortable, like something may be waiting for me on the other side. I push them gently, but they open with a jolt. There is nothing on the other side but for the stairwell that's always been there. I've rarely paid attention to it in the past, though I never recall it looking as dark as it does today. There is a second set of fire doors about fifteen feet away. These are doors I definitely never recall having noticed before; though if I have, I certainly never saw them closed like they are now.

I walk into the stairwell, and the fire doors close behind me. The air is dead. The overhead light flickers. I need to get to the next set of doors, but I can't; I am frozen and I'm standing there and I'm feeling like an idiot. And then boom, I hear a voice.

"Could you come with us please?"

The voice seems to be coming from deep in the recesses of my brain, but maybe it's coming from the stairwell? I just don't know. I hadn't seen anyone there, but it's so dark and I haven't been paying attention. I feel so cold. I do not respond.

"There's nothing to worry about."

I know the voice is not to be trusted, but I do not know why. I still do not respond. I don't move at all. It's in my head. I know it. And I start saying to myself over and over again, not real, not real, not real.

"C'mon buddy, we just want to talk."

At this point I start thinking, if this is not real, and if I haven't done anything, then I can leave, ending this whenever I want. And yet I can't quite get myself to move. Is it that I'm too scared or too intrigued? If it is in my head do I somehow feel responsible, nay obligated to follow this path wherever it might go? Maybe. Sure. I don't know. I push on the second set of doors.

"So, how are you doing?" J. asks at the next session.

"How am I doing?" I say. "Fine, good, all right. It's funny though…" and I explain to him the story of the fire doors, J. just nodding the whole time. "Anyway, I'm frozen and standing there," I'm telling him. "And I hear this voice asking me to come with it somewhere. Like I've done something, something I need to be punished for. Like I'm Josef K. or some other fucked-up character like that. The voice tells me not to worry. But how can't I worry? I will myself to open that second set of doors, and even though I can breathe again after I do, it's just another empty hallway on the other side, the paranoia lingers and it's still lingering, and it's all so crazy."

"Why do you think this is," J. says, "and what have you been thinking about?"

"I've been thinking about being stuck between those doors and not being able to get out. That instead of just being able to leave, I'm thrown into a small, windowless room for questioning, and how I would like to think that I wouldn't know what was going on, but I would. And then I would be asked to recount my conversation with you, but I wouldn't be able to, not exactly, not the same way I had just done it, because I knew even then how fucked up it was that I would have to come before you again this week. How I would not be able to talk about my friend, his lost love, his reunion and how someone is supposed to deal with that, because that was a lie. And while I really don't want to think about this stuff unless I'm here, I don't even really want to do that. I would rather lie to you, and keep lying to you.

"Thing is, though, those doors, those fucking doors got in the way, they wouldn't let me leave, and now what? Am I supposed to think about this all the time? Am I supposed to leave Alice and my kids? Is that it? And for what, someone I haven't seen in twenty years, and something that's going to last for six months? And then what, I'll be that guy, that guy who was just talking shit? You know. That guy who said he was never going to be that guy, that guy that leaves his family and fucks everything up? Fuck that. Fuck me. Fuck."

"Okay, good, let's talk about this," J. says.

Panties

IT WAS AUGUST, and Charlie and Stephanie were on a double date with Chris and Jenny. Chris and Jenny had set them up and they had gone to the Airport Drive-In, the one up on the hill, just past the Oakdale Mall, and not so coincidentally near the Two Rivers Airport.

Charlie was of average height, and just less than average self-esteem, but funny, and Stephanie had long dark hair and legs that went on forever. Charlie had a decent rapport with the ladies, but he could never close the deal; something always went wrong. Sometimes he said too much, other times the wrong thing, and lot of the time he just seemed needy. It's nice to be wanted, but not too much, and not too desperately at that. And while Charlie knew this, it didn't prevent him from pushing too hard, too often.

Charlie and Stephanie had climbed into the trunk about a half-mile away from the drive-in so they could sneak in to the movie. "So you come here often?" Charlie said, just centimeters away from Stephanie and too nervous not too speak.

"Is that your idea of a pick-up line?" Stephanie said, playing along.

"Not my best one," Charlie said, "but it seemed most appropriate."

"What else do you have?" Stephanie said.

"How about, if I told you had a great body would you hold it against me?" Charlie said.

"Better," Stephanie said. "Keep going."

Both of Charlie's arms were starting to fall asleep, and as he went to adjust them his right hand landed on Stephanie's hip and his left hand brushed against her right breast.

"I didn't say you were doing that well," Stephanie said, "but you are growing on me."

"Pardon me," Charlie said, flushed with embarrassment.

"I didn't mean it that way," Stephanie said, "but now that you mention it, is that a pack of Rolos in your pocket, or are you just happy to be stuck in a trunk with me?"

Charlie paused, beads of sweat now dotting his upper lip. Stephanie was interested, clearly interested, and he was doing amazingly well, the close quarters somehow enhancing his confidence.

Stephanie stared at him, and he knew that this was his chance. Charlie leaned in for the kiss, and Stephanie arched her neck, opening her mouth just slightly, waiting, and ready, caught up in the moment.

The trunk popped open. "We're here," Chris said. "I hope I didn't interrupt anything."

"Yeah, no," Charlie said. "Not quite."

Charlie and Stephanie climbed into the backseat of Chris' car. Stephanie was wearing a short denim skirt and her legs splayed out across the seat. Her thighs were a rich almond brown and Charlie soon found himself transfixed with Stephanie's every movement—the crossing and uncrossing of her legs, the occasional thigh-on-thigh contact, the undulations of the little freckles dancing above her knees.

And then he saw her panties, stark white, cotton, and set against her dark thighs. They were a vision, coursing with electricity and intoxicating, like the sail of a great ship. They beckoned him and spoke to him—*touch me, touch me now*—and like a salmon swimming back upstream to spawn, Charlie was drawn to them, entranced by powers far stronger then he could ever hope to resist.

Charlie started to reach for them, his hand extending to this promised and mysterious land. He was so close, so sure of himself. This was where he was supposed to go. His hand slowly snaked between Stephanie's legs and then disappeared from view. Charlie was convinced that he was in the clear. He could practically taste her panties now. And then Stephanie shifted and he felt her warm thighs close around his hand.

"Jesus Christ," Stephanie said. "What are you doing, you fucking perv?"

Charlie snapped out of his reverie, the spell broken. He suddenly remembered where he was, and as Stephanie began to move away from him, Charlie knew that just as five more minutes in the trunk might have led to something great, this little escapade had blown any chance of his ever seeing those panties on the floor of his room or anywhere else.

Charlie looked up at the movie, and as Julia Roberts drunkenly kissed someone, woke up hung over, and regretted it, but not exactly, he wondered what might have been.

Charlie realized that he and Stephanie might have kissed as well at some point later that night. A soft, crunchy first kiss that lingered forever, her lips parting just a touch, inviting Charlie to flick his tongue in and out of her moist and scrumptious mouth, even as his hands moved from her shoulders down to her hips, where he would stop momentarily, before sliding them up her stomach and onto her breasts for a brief grope and twist, before finally cupping her face for the big finale.

That kiss would have led to others, of course, and at some point Charlie would have even touched the panties he so strongly craved. Stephanie would have started using some of his closet space and he would have given her a set of his keys. They would have started to talk long into night about having children, a boy and a girl, Jack and Diane, "like the song" they would explain to others while laughing, and a dog, a chocolate brown Lab named Snappy who would nip at everyone's heels.

They would have been married at dusk on the beach in Hawaii, and Charlie would have gotten a little too drunk and tried to kiss Stephanie's hot, weirdo younger sister Fern. This would have caused some tension at the time, but they would all laugh about it later. They would have joked about how they would all pose for holiday photos some day that Stephanie would then send out along with the family newsletter, updating anyone and everyone who cared about that year's struggles and triumphs.

Charlie would go on to work at IBM and Stephanie would take a few years off to raise Jack and Diane, only to later obtain her real estate license after they were both safely off to school. Charlie would flirt with his almost-too-young-to-be-legal assistant over after work drinks at Thirsty's, but never quite go all the way, while Stephanie would lust after Jerry another salesman at her company, but never breathe a word of it to him or anyone else.

Jack would have some drinking problems and get kicked out of not one, but two colleges. He'd find God at some point, however, and sober up, and though Charlie and Stephanie would always wonder if maybe he'd gone just a little crazy, they would have to admit that he seemed awfully chipper and fulfilled.

Diane would experiment sexually throughout college—boys, girls, and endless combinations thereof—before spending a couple of years after college living in a commune in New Mexico with her bald, Asian-American girlfriend Dee. After that "phase" came to an end, she would move home, marry her high-school boyfriend Bobby; and though she would never feel quite fulfilled, it was a life and not a bad one that.

Charlie and Stephanie would go on and on, through strokes, heart attacks, good times and bad. They would retire to New Hampshire together and go birding when the weather was good and Charlie's sciatica wasn't acting up. Stephanie would pass one night in her sleep, peacefully, as they like to say, and Charlie would go a few weeks later, loneliness the likely culprit.

It was a whole life born of two people thrown into a trunk together, but it was not to be; the panties had seen to that. Charlie briefly weighed what he might say to Stephanie to try and win her back—"I mean, you've seen your panties, haven't you, what else could I do?"—but thought the better of it and turned his attention back to the movie, as Julia Roberts prepared to marry the guy she supposedly regretted kissing.

Just Like That

I AM HEADING TO WORK. It's early and Claire is still asleep. When I hit the breezeway I realize that I forgot my keys. I walk back into the house and start rustling through the junk on the table by the door. After a moment I sense someone standing behind me and then see their ghostly reflection in the window that faces the woods in back of the house.

I turn around to look at Mark, who I haven't seen in quite some time. He is disoriented and looks like hell. His skin is sallow, his hair is thin and wispy, and his dull and lifeless eyes have sunk far back into his skull.

"Hey, man," I say, forcing a smile. "What are you doing here?"

Mark steadies himself by putting a hand on the table and then purses his lips, trying to form words that seem to get lost somewhere in his mouth before they can emerge.

"I-I-I was coming home from Thirsty's," he stammers, "and I saw your door was open. I came in to close it, because that's not safe."

"Thanks, man. I'm here, though, and Claire is still asleep," I say, seeing a small twitch on his otherwise placid face as I mention her name. "So it's cool, okay?"

"Yeah, sure," he says, and then he wanders out into the morning light.

The first time I really spoke to Mark, we were in fifth grade and he was standing in front of his house on Brookfield, stepping on caterpillars and watching their greenish-yellow insides ooze across the sidewalk. I didn't know him well. His dad was a local cop who was always drunk, and his mom was a hottie who obsessively ran laps down at the track next to MacArthur, the elementary school we went to. Mark didn't have friends that I knew of, but on this day he seemed cool and weird and I couldn't help but silently stare at him as he went about his business.

"Hey, you got a bike?" he suddenly said, turning to face me.

"Yeah," I said.

"Cool. Let's ride to Two Rivers Plaza and get some candy."

I had never ridden my bike all the way to Two Rivers Plaza, and while I wasn't sure I was even allowed to, no one was home to say no. As we started to ride I realized that I was kind of scared. I knew, though, that if my dad had been there and not running around with whoever he was seeing at the moment, he would have told me to suck it up, that fear was for pussies. He also would have been right; because as it turned out, we did not find ourselves pedaling to the edge of the world, nor were there dragons waiting to fight us when we got to the plaza. We didn't even see any adults we knew.

"I don't have any money, do you?" Mark said after we parked our bikes.

"No," I said, realizing I hadn't thought of that.

"Don't sweat it," he said. "We can just shoplift."

"I don't know," I said. I had never stolen anything.

"It's really easy," Mark said.

"Okay," I said, "but how do you do it?"

"You grab what you want and then walk through the store saying, 'Mom, where are you, can I get this' and you walk right out the back door."

"Just like that?" I said.

"Yup."

And it was just like that. Day after day we stole candy, baseball cards, copies of MAD magazine, and shit we didn't even want, just because we could. And it was glorious, until it wasn't.

We were leaving the store one afternoon when Mark and I each felt a hand clamp down on our shoulders. We looked up to see a guy with greasy, side-parted hair staring down at us and smiling madly, a mix of glee and malevolence. "I've been waiting to catch you little faggots in the act," he said. "Come with me."

We were marched into an airless back room, empty but for an old desk and two folding chairs. There were no windows. "Sit down, boys," the guy said as he closed the door. "And tell me, who's the ringleader here?"

We didn't answer him.

"Not talking," he continued. "All right, I can always call your fathers."

I looked at the guy in his ill-fitting shirt and polyester slacks. If all he had was the dad threat, I knew he couldn't do shit. We could ride this out. We just needed to be tough.

I looked over at Mark. He was sniffling.

"What's up, slick," the guy said to Mark. "You don't want me to speak to your dad?"

"No, please," Mark said now, blubbering and practically falling off of his chair.

"What about you," the guy said, turning his attention to me.

"How do you feel about me calling your dad?"

I looked over at Mark again, who was still crying, and saw in his eyes that he was imploring me to beg the guy not to. I recognized that this was a moment when friends, real friends, acted in a certain way. That this was about character, something my dad liked to stress the importance of when he was actually around. My dad also said, though, that crying was a sign of weakness, and while he could tolerate a lot of things, weakness was not one of them.

"Go ahead," I said, ignoring Mark and calling the guy's bluff. "You think I care what my dad thinks?"

The guy did a brief double-take, recovered, and then took a moment to just stare at us. "All right, then," the guy finally said. "How's this? You guys don't come into the store for one year, and if you do, I call your dads, got it?"

"Got it," Mark said, jumping up to shake the guy's hand.

We left the store and walked into the sunlight. Mark ran his sleeve across his tear-streaked cheeks, looked at me sadly, and then jumped onto his bike and rode away.

Claire and I go to breakfast early one Sunday morning at the Park Diner and then start the walk back home, past the carwash and up along the overpass and down by the Hess Station. As we cross Vestal Avenue we come up to a muffler shop where the Pudgie's Pizza used to be when we were kids. It's cool and damp out, but fresh and crisp as well, with fall looming somewhere off beyond South Mountain. As we start to walk up Pennsylvania Avenue we see Mark lying in the street alongside the curb. He is trying to gain his balance, one hand on the curb, one reaching for heights far beyond his limited range of motion. He cannot get up, though; and as he looks in our direction we see he is silently pleading for someone, anyone, to help him. We don't move. We are frozen and unsure of what to do. Mark teeters for a moment and then falls to the street, no chance of getting back up.

We look at him one more time, and then averting our eyes we walk past him, not once looking back.

It is the worst thing we've ever done.

Well, that's not true. It's the second worst.

Mark and I don't have much contact after the shoplifting incident. I know about him, though. He is the first kid to raid his parents' liquor cabinet and the first to take Dexatrim after he hears that eating a whole box is just like taking speed. He is also the first to sneak into the Pine Lounge on the west side and get served; and by the time we are seniors he is the most famous drunk in our school, someone you can count on to comes to class intoxicated, throw up at parties and pass out on the front lawn. He is also with Claire, whose parents, like Mark's, are barely there even when they are there.

One night, I hold a party at my house and Mark and Claire come by. Once there, Mark proceeds to do tap counts from the half-keg we have rolled into the backyard. When he is done, he stumbles into the woods and then collapses onto the bed of leaves below, where he sleeps throughout the night sheltered by the trees above.

At some point almost everyone has gone home, except for Claire who doesn't seem to have anywhere to go. I have never talked to Claire nor have I ever noticed how beautiful her eyes were. Until tonight.

"You're pretty quiet," she says.

"Maybe you don't know me," I say.

"I don't know anybody," she says.

"You know Mark," I say.

"You used to know him," she says. "What happened?"

"I don't know. People grow apart, I guess, and then they move on."

"I think I want to move on," she says.

"Yeah?"

"Yeah, but I don't want to be alone," she says. "I need somewhere I can go to."

"Okay, where then? Where's that going to be?"

"How about here," she said, "with you?"

"Just like that," I say.

"Just like that," she says.

For a moment, just a moment, I think again about character and weakness and about how my dad has always stressed that being a man means never going after another man's woman. I also wonder where he is tonight and who he's with.

One morning, I am walking out of CVS with Josh, my three-year old son with Claire. It's just the two of us, and we are happy and goofing off, thinking about lunch and how maybe we should watch Barney when we get home. As we turn onto Vestal Avenue I see Mark standing on the sidewalk. He is unsteady on his feet and wildly flailing his arms. I take Josh's hand, wondering how this is going to play out. Mark then looks at us, points his finger at me and starts to shout.

"You mock me like this," he shouts. "You throw your life in my face."

He looks stricken and I don't know what to do or say, so I pull on Josh's wrist and drag him across the street.

As I look back, I see that Mark is flailing his arms again. I also see that the sun is now slicing between the Garrett's Hardware and CVS, enveloping him in the soft, hazy afternoon glow, and briefly illuminating him as he rages about things I will never understand.

Never Said

WE'RE AT THE PARK DINER. My dad Tommie is sitting across from me. He looks haggard, tired. His skin is pasty and washed-out. He's not talking, so I'm not talking either, but it doesn't matter because it's hanging there between us.

Cancer.

Motherfucker.

"Don't look so upset, kid," my dad finally says. "It's going to be fine."

I look away so he won't notice that I'm crying, and I see the painting of Icarus across the room. The painting has been there forever which means that Icarus has been falling forever as well, no respite in sight.

"What's next?" I ask.

"I could go home and die," my dad says. "One doctor already suggested that. Or I can try this new experimental trial they're starting at Two Rivers General."

I don't say anything.

"Look bud, I'm past normal shit—it's experimental or nothing at this point. But there's this hot-shot doctor that just moved here and he's bringing the trial with him."

I'm still at a loss. How am I supposed to react to something like this? Especially since I have spent a significant chunk of my life hating him and hoping he would die.

"Okay, don't talk," he says. "I'll be at the Oncology Unit at Two Rivers at eleven tomorrow morning if you want to join me. If you don't, though, I get it."

What does he get? That he left and came home only to leave again, endlessly repeating this cycle the whole time I was growing up? That my mom finally had to leave him, but that she came back too? That things never really changed, but that when she was dying from uterine cancer, he lovingly took care of her like none of it ever happened and so I owe him something regardless of my other feelings?

Fuck.

"I'll be there," I say. "You know I'll be there."

When I get to Two Rivers General the next morning I have to cross through the room where everyone is being treated. It is white and stark, sterile and without life. Well, except for the people there. They are of all ages, and they all have one thing in common, IVs hanging out of their arms that are trying to battle some unknown assailant that is only too eager and too equipped to wipe out a lifetime of memories, screw-ups and regrets.

As I enter the main office I see that my father is already sitting down across from the doctor, who looks both terribly young and terribly familiar to me though I can't quite place him. There's something about him, though; I know him from somewhere, somewhere a long time ago.

"Hey man," the doctor says, practically jumping over his desk when he sees me. "How are you doing?"

"What, you guys know each other?" my dad says.

"Yeah, we went to high school together, though he may not remember me," the doctor says. "William Knox. Uh, Billy Knox."

Holy shit, of course—Billy fucking Knox, the D&D super-dweeb who grew up down the street from us on South Mountain. We went to school together from kindergarten through high-school graduation, and I probably never said more than ten words to him in total that whole time. I had heard he went to Princeton, that he had been a Rhodes Scholar or something, and that he was a hot-shot at Merck now. Damn.

"Yeah, of course," I say. "Billy Knox. What brings you home?"

"I...I mean we...we really wanted to raise our kids here," Billy says. "Frankie and I."

Frankie Hill, the cheerleader? Bullshit.

"You remember Frankie Hill, right?" he asks a little too eagerly.

Do I remember Frankie Hill? And how smoking hot she was in high school? Of course I do. And Billy's awfully proud of himself for bagging her. It's probably even more important to him right here, right now, than being a big-time doctor. He wants to show off and I ought to let him. But I don't.

"Uh, yeah," I say. "Cheerleader, right? I think I sort of remember her."

He recoils a bit, but then plows ahead. He needs this. "Right, anyway, I was home for the weekend a couple of years ago, and I saw her across the bar at the Pine and it just sort of clicked," he says, grinning. So now he's one up on me and there's nothing more to discuss.

Frankie Hill was from the east side of town. She was sort of trashy, and sort of awesome, with her curly blonde '80s hair and acid-washed jeans. We had actually hooked up one time at a party. It had been drunken and hot and I thought for sure that I was going to fuck her. I'm not sure what happened, though; I was so close, but I couldn't close the deal. Anyway, it was a long time ago and Billy doesn't need to know about that. Still, I wonder what she looks like now. And what the fuck she's doing with Billy. Crazy.

"That's great," I say. "Please say hello for me."

"Yeah, yeah of course," he says.

"And me," my dad says. "Sorry to break up the reunion here."

"Sorry," Billy says. "That was unprofessional of me. It's just so weird being home. Lots of memories. Back to work though. I expect this to be pretty straightforward. We'll run some tests this morning, we'll check the numbers this afternoon and it should be a slam dunk. This is a miracle drug and we need bodies to prove it."

"When would we start?" my dad asks.

"We can start tomorrow morning," Billy says. "Two weeks of radiation and then chemo infused with our drug for two weeks after that. Cool?"

"Yeah," I say, "very cool."

"Good. Be in by 9:30. We'll finalize some paperwork and then get to it."

"And that's it," my dad says.

"Yup. I'm the boss, and what I say goes," Billy says with an authority he is only showing for the first time since we arrived.

After the test my dad and I hit Thirsty's for a round of beers to celebrate his good luck. One round leads to another, and then some shots, and at some point I start thinking about Frankie Hill, our brief time together and my lost opportunity. I was so close and so into it and she just wasn't. At first she was, and then I don't know, I fumbled, and it's funny how quickly you can fall back into thinking about the mistakes you made. But there I am doing just that until some brunette in a short dress walks by, and we buy another round and head out to her car, and I'm on top of her, and thinking about

Frankie, and then I'm waking up on my couch, still fully dressed from the night before, and it's 9:20 and I am about to be really late for my dad's first day of the trial.

When I get to Two Rivers General, I sprint through the Oncology Unit and past all the people with their IVs, noting that my dad is not among them. I get to Billy's office and Billy is there, but my dad isn't.

"Hey Billy," I say, doubled over and trying to catch my breath. "Where's my dad? Is he being prepped or what?"

Billy doesn't respond at first. He looks very stiff and formal and nothing like the day before. "I have a question I'd like to ask you first," he says.

"Yeah? What?"

"You remember Frankie better than you let on, don't you? I spoke to her about you last night when I got home."

"Sure, okay, sort of. But it was a long time ago and it was nothing, and I didn't think I should mention it. Don't sweat it, dude, you got her and that's awesome. Look, where's my dad?"

"She says you forced yourself on her. That she thought it was something more casual. That nothing happened, but that she was scared, that she wanted you to stop and you didn't want to, not at first. Is that true?"

"No way," I say, because that isn't true, is it? No, not really, though even as I say this I get a flash of her face, her scared face that night, and me wanting to push her for a moment, a long moment, but just a moment. "That's not how I remember it at all. We were drunk, we hooked up, and I stopped pushing as soon as she asked me to. I think there's a misunderstanding here."

"Okay, whatever. Thing is, I sent your dad home. We can't help him. Once we examined him, we realized that he's too old and he's much too sick."

I feel like I've been punched in the stomach. "What?" I say. "You didn't mention that any of this was a possibility yesterday."

"No?" Billy says. "That's odd. Maybe I was distracted. Still, we have a strict protocol here, and I'm sorry I wasn't clear about that."

He's lying, or at least bending the truth. And I'm falling. I need to push back. "There's something wrong about this," I say, wanting to hear something unexpected. But I know what's coming.

"Maybe you just remember things differently than I do," he says. "Maybe it's just a misunderstanding."

"And so what can we do now?" I ask.

"Nothing," Billy says, turning away. "I'm sorry it didn't work out like you wanted it to."

Goddess

"SO, DO YOU STILL THINK I'M HOT? I mean, do you think men still find me attractive?" Jenny asks.

This is never a good question to entertain, much less answer. I know this as surely as I know anything. Still, let's break it down.

I am married.

Jenny is married.

There is history.

I know her husband Robby.

Robby has a violent streak.

And Jenny is not all there anymore.

And yet, I have wanted to fuck her since high school, and so maybe we could get together on the sly. No feelings involved. No strings attached. No nothing. Just sex.

"C'mon," Jenny says. "It's just a question. You don't have to read anything more into it than that."

She says this as we sit in a booth in the back corner of Thirsty's.

She says this while staring into my eyes, her hand now resting on my shoulder and knowing there's history. She remembers that, doesn't she?

We're in high school, senior year, and Jenny is a goddess, an untouchable goddess with a brown bob haircut, freckles, crazy green eyes and ridiculous soccer calves. Everyone wants her, not just me, though maybe no one wants her more than me, something she knows all too well.

She and Robby, though, they've been together since eighth grade and nothing is going to change that, regardless of how many other girls he bangs. It's a love story. Jenny is the beauty and Robby is the beast. We're all friends, but it doesn't change the fact that he is a behemoth; a football-playing, head-smashing, unhinged behemoth.

Now, does that mean Robby goes around beating people up? No, it doesn't; because one, if it doesn't involve Jenny he doesn't really care, and two, he knows what he's capable of when he's enraged, and he would rather avoid having anyone else end up like Jimmy Woods. Jimmy Woods thought it would be funny to provoke Robby when we were in ninth grade, and egg him on from behind as we waited in line to go into school.

"What's up, you big retard? How's the weather up there?"

It was stupid shit like that, mostly, stuff Robby could ignore. But then Jimmy fucked up.

"Yo, Robby, did Jenny tell you how I fingered her on Saturday night? It was sweet."

Robby didn't say a word. He just turned around and punched Jimmy as hard as he could in the mouth. Did Robby realize he would knock out six of Jimmy's teeth? Or break his jaw? Who knows? But did anyone mess with him after that, or even bother to talk to Jenny? No, never.

And yet does this mean I am not supposed to find Jenny attractive? Or wonder what might have happened if I had gotten to her before

Robby? Might we be together? Does Jenny ever think about this as well? I think she does. I definitely want to believe so, anyway.

Which is why, despite everything, I let myself sneak off with her at parties; never making a move, just hoping to lose myself in those eyes, and that smile, if only for a little bit. It is also why I am in the kitchen with her at Judy's party near the end of senior year, and pretending to listen as she talks about some soccer game against some other high school.

"And then..." she says, then pauses. "Hey, are you even listening to me?"

"I am, really. Go on."

"Yeah?" she says, smiling. "What did I just say?"

I can try to lie here. I don't. "No idea," I say.

"I thought so. So, look, can I ask you something?"

"Sure, what?"

"Well, you know Robby and I have been together since like eighth grade, right?"

"Right."

"And it's great."

"Okay."

"But you know, sometimes I wonder what I've missed, and I guess, I don't know, do you think other guys find me attractive?"

She puts her hand on my shoulder as she says this. Fuck. I should deflect this question. Or, something, but I can't. I want her, and maybe this is an opening.

"Are you kidding?" I say. "You're gorgeous. And so cool. Anyone would be thrilled to be with you."

"Anyone," she says, leaning forward.

I pause. I look at her. I close my eyes and lean in as well.

Bam!

Something, or someone, has hit me in the kidneys from behind.

I can't breathe. I am lying on the kitchen floor. I can't see Jenny anymore, but I can see Robby and he is looming over me and smiling, and then dragging Jenny out of the house. I should get up and chase them, defend her, maybe. Do something. But instead I lie there, feeling sorry for myself and thinking about lost opportunities, as opposed to what Jenny may or may not be going through.

I don't see Jenny for a week. No one does. There are rumors of a black eye, maybe an accident, but nothing more. She comes back to school, finishing quietly, no more parties, no more late-night conversations, just Jenny and Robby, Robby and Jenny, graduating, and leaving for college together, off to some small school where no one knows them.

Some of us leave home and come back. Some of us never leave. No one knows much about Robby and Jenny, though. We hear rumors that they're married, that they live in Colorado, no, New Mexico, maybe Michigan, that they have kids, that he's an engineer, no, something with software maybe, and Jenny, no one knows, not for sure anyway.

Meanwhile, we have our own families, and raise our own children, who go to the schools we went to. And when we're not eating pizza at Mario's or manicotti at Little Venice, attending parent-teacher conferences at MacArthur or Thomas Jefferson, working, or hanging out at Oquaga Lake, we drink at Thirsty's. We always have Thirsty's.

It is at Thirsty's when we hear that Robby and Jenny are coming home. Someone spoke to someone who sold them a house. Robby's mom is sick. His company doesn't care where he works. They want to raise their kids where they were raised. After all these years they want to come home.

There are rumors, of course. Jenny apparently has some low-level type of brain damage, nothing terribly noticeable, some memory stuff, maybe, some emotional moments, but all of it subtle. There had been a car accident, which may be the real reason they are coming home, because Robby can't care for Jenny himself, or won't. No one knows for sure what's true, though. Just like no one knows if it really was an accident, or if maybe it was a fight and Robby actually pushed Jenny out of the car.

When I initially hear all of this, it doesn't occur to me that I've been thinking about Jenny in the back of my head all these years. Not as I got married, or as I have tried to hang onto a marriage that is fine enough, but stale. I'm pretty sure I've never looked at other women either, but now that I know I'm going to see Jenny again and talk to her, I start wondering if we will be able to steal away and pick up where we left off that night in the kitchen. Soon it is all that I can think about. Well, that and whether I am part of the reason she wanted to come home.

And now here we are. At first, all I can think about is sleeping with her. But the more we talk, the more tired she seems, and the more desperate. And maybe it's my imagination, but maybe it's not. She's also not really as beautiful as I remembered her being. And maybe she does seem a little off, because she's definitely gripping my shoulder a little too tightly, which is maybe making me feel a little trapped.

"So do you find me attractive," she says again, "or what?"

"I-I-I don't know," I stammer.

"You don't know. C'mon. What the fuck?"

I see Robby across the room, laughing, lumbering around, big and loud, always big and loud. I look into Jenny's eyes, which are no longer so green, and are actually sort of gray and sort of dead, and lacking any kind of spark. I also see the traces of crow's feet creeping out below her temples, and the way her jaw sags when she leans forward.

She seems so sad and beaten down; and maybe this is my imagination as well, maybe, but I am really not looking to be a hero, I never was. And either way, this definitely isn't what I was hoping for when I hoped we would find a moment together.

"C'mon," she says. "This isn't right. Please say something. Anything."

There are probably a lot of things I could say, but I don't. Instead I get up, I head towards the door, and I don't look back.

No Nothing

I LOOK AT HIM across the pool table. He's trying to line up his shot, but his hands are shaking and he's unstable on his feet. It occurs to me that I could put my coffee down and walk over to him. I could grasp him by his shoulders or grip his elbow, offering him support so he could actually take a shot. I even picture myself doing this.

But I don't do it. I don't move. I watch him struggle, and while I am not exactly enjoying myself, I'm also not feeling anything. Not what I could be feeling anyway.

Fuck him.

He takes his shot, the pool cue sliding off of his finger and skidding across the table, the chalk dust curling into the light before drifting away.

My dad shakes his head and smiles. "Can you believe that shit?" he says before taking a seat.

I don't say anything.

"You hate me," he says sadly.

Do I hate him?

No, no I don't.

Should I hate him for leaving my mom and me, for preferring bars to little league games, and for being so sick now after a mostly wasted life?

I don't know. I'm way past caring about that stuff.

What about the time he checked himself out of Two Rivers General and walked barefoot all the way to my high school, just to wait for me in his rumpled suit and bloody feet as everyone was leaving for the day, hoping to borrow a few dollars? Do I hate him for that?

No, not anymore. I'm numb to that. Numb to him. No feelings. No nothing. I feel nothing.

"I'm dying," my dad says to me.

He looks like hell. Old and beat-up, his cheeks all sharp angles and just barely holding on to the sagging skin that looks like it's trying to desperately escape his face.

"So you keep telling me," I finally say.

"No Petey boy, this is different," he says.

"Man, you will make up any excuse you can when you're shooting poorly," I say, wanting to avoid this conversation. "It's embarrassing. You are embarrassed about that, right?"

"All right kid," he says. "How about you get me home? I'm tired."

I drive him back to his building. We are silent. He pauses by my window, looks like he's going to say something, and then shuffles away.

Sirens are going off. Or maybe it's an air raid, like when we were kids and were told to hide under our desks just in case the Russians ever decided to bomb us. I try to adjust, and then roll out of bed, realizing it's the phone and it's the middle of the night, and no one ever calls in the middle of the night for good reasons.

"Hello?" I say.

It's Two Rivers General. It's the call I've been expecting for hours.

I'm at the funeral home. Scotty Dooley Jr. is sitting across from me. Scotty Dooley Jr. is a rich kid from the west side and a smug prick who now works in the family business. We went to high school together and he knows who my dad is. Scotty Jr. and his dad, Scotty Sr., probably saw my dad sleeping outside of the Park Diner after coming home from church, or scrounging for drink money at Tom & Marty's when things were at their worst.

Scotty Jr. has always looked down on me and I've taken it, I had to; my dad is who he is and there's no denying it. Of course now Scotty Jr. is burying my dad, and that just sucks.

"I'm sorry about your dad," he says with his perfect hair and perfect teeth, never looking up from the papers on his desk.

Bullshit, I think to myself. "Thanks," I say.

"Let's talk coffins," Scotty Jr. says. "There are a number of possibilities."

I am about to break his heart, something that offers me some joy. "You know," I say, "I'm going to build the coffin myself."

"What? How? That's not how this usually works. There are laws," he says.

"From what I understand," I say, lying through my teeth, "you just need to give me your permission. Do I have it?"

"I need to talk to my dad." Scotty Jr. walks out of the room and into another office, where I hear muffled voices and occasional words like "drunk" and "loser."

Scotty comes back in with his fake weatherman smile. "That's cool," he says, "but we'll need it by tomorrow morning."

"Fine," I say.

I go to the lumber yard to buy the wood I need, and then stop by Giant on the way home for a case of Yuengling. I spend the night in my garage sanding, planing and assembling the coffin. I try not to think about how much I worried about my dad as a kid, or how I endlessly sat on the couch by the window, waiting for him to come home. I also try not to think about how much I have tried not to think about these things as an adult.

By morning there is a coffin and by afternoon there is a funeral. Hardly anyone is there; just me, some cousin I don't know, a drinking buddy of my dad who leaves as soon as he learns there will not be refreshments, and Scotty Jr., who is standing in the back and trying to look professional.

The gravesite is on a hill, under a tree, the Susquehanna River off in the distance. It's very pleasant and kind of grand, and on the one hand it's better than my dad deserves; but standing here now, like this, with him gone, I can't help but feel like he deserved a better life as well. He didn't want to be an alcoholic or a sorta crappy father. He didn't plan to get cancer, so why shouldn't he get some peace now that it's all over?

Scotty Jr. tells me that the stone won't be done for a couple of days, but that I have no need to worry; he will personally see to it that it gets finished. He then drifts off and I am by myself.

I get the last six-pack of Yuengling from my car and drink one beer after another, standing over my dad's grave as the sun slowly sets and day becomes night. I do not cry. Not one drop. I won't give the old man that. No emotion. No nothing.

The days pass and I don't get back to the grave. A couple of months later, though, I wander out to the cemetery, thinking about how peaceful the site was and how nice it would be to drink a couple of beers there. When I get to the grave I pop open a Yuengling and take a long, cold swallow, my eyes watering up. As I wipe away the tears, I look down at the stone and see that my dad's name is spelled wrong. Even in death he's been fucked.

I call Scotty Jr.

"Hello," he says.

"Hey, man," I say, trying to stay disengaged. "My dad's name is misspelled on his stone."

"Yeah, I'm sorry about that, we'll fix it as soon as we can. We're really busy right now, though. Is next week cool?"

Is he kidding? "No," I say, trying to stay calm, surprised that I am starting to feel angry. "It isn't cool. Show some respect."

"Right, of course. Friday?"

"Look, I already paid for it," my voice starting to strain. "C'mon. What the fuck."

"Cool, all right, tomorrow. It'll be fixed tomorrow."

I come back the next day and it's not fixed. I feel nothing. I want to feel nothing.

I call Scotty and get his secretary. Scotty doesn't call back. Nothing.

I call him back. He leaves me a voicemail when I miss his call. "Wednesday for sure. Cool?"

Wednesday comes and goes. My head starts to hurt, and a pain like nothing I have ever felt before starts to inch its way up along the back of my neck.

I go to the cemetery. No change. No nothing. I know what I need to do, and knowing it is oddly calming.

I call Scotty and get his voicemail. "Hey, man," I say as calmly as I can muster. "If you're not here within two hours to fix this, I'm going to come to your office and beat the shit out of you. And then when I'm done I'm going to beat the shit out of your dad, then beat the shit out of your mom if she's there, and then beat the shit out of anyone else who happens to work for you. Cool?"

And then I wait there by the grave, drinking beer and praying all the while that he doesn't make it on time.

.

After the Flood
2014

"And what did you hear, my darling young one? I heard the sound of a thunder that roared out a warnin'"

—"A Hard Rain's A-Gonna Fall," Bob Dylan

How It Works

THERE IS NO CLAIRE. It's true that she doesn't always come home. It's also true that I stopped worrying about that a while ago. Still, this is different. There's a storm coming and what if she can't get home, but wants to? Then what?

"Storm's coming," Claire said.

"So," I said.

"So, they say it will be the storm of the century," she said.

"And," I said, knowing she wanted to leave and would find any excuse she could to do so.

"We may need stuff, food, or cigarettes, alcohol," she said.

"We have tequila," I said.

"It's not enough," she said.

And I suppose that's the rub. Nothing is enough anymore, not me certainly.

"Go ahead," I said, grabbing her shoulders and staring into her dead eyes.

"What?" she said.

"Everything is fucked," I said.

"That's the storm talking," she said. "End of the world shit. Let it go."

So I do. I let it go, and then I let her go. But she never quite came back.

I stop thinking about Claire.

Instead, when the rain starts I close my windows and roll my car into the garage. As the thunder begins to crack, then sizzle, and the air turns green, I put my feet up on the ottoman and I open the shades to better enjoy the view. While the tree branches sway, bend, then splinter, and the skies begin to swirl and twist, I open the bottle of tequila. I pour a shot, and keep pouring, as the house begins to shake and threatens to become unmoored from the foundation I poured with my father so long ago.

After things go black I shift to drinking straight from the bottle, the golden liquid splashing onto my beard, chest, and lap. I see the crunchy worm swimming towards me with every burning gulp and I decide that with so little to care about, it's a gift to have anything to look forward to. The rain continues its rat-tat-tat assault on my windows and roof, and as the worm slides, then lands on my tongue, I pause, savoring the moment and embracing the possibility that this just may be the end of the world.

After that I bite the worm.

My father once told me that stealing another man's woman was the most pussy thing a man could do. It was like murdering him. That never stopped my father though. Nor did it stop me. Of course I never did listen to him. Something I find myself thinking about the night Claire and I are drinking at Thirsty's and we run into Mark.

We didn't expect to see Mark, but to expect something is to think about it, and we hadn't thought about him in a long time.

He was no more sober than I remembered him, but something seemed different. Age is funny like that, though. Things no longer make sense in the same way. It's like with an Etch-a-Sketch. One minute that which you so carefully created is right there in front of you, and then it gets shaken, and suddenly it's gone, just like that.

After another pitcher, though, I realize what's different. It's not him, he's the same. It's us. We've changed, we stopped caring, and in no longer caring we are no longer better than Mark, though maybe we never were. He had loved Claire and she had run to me, his former friend, and I welcomed her, with open arms, and no consideration of what was right.

But now here we were together again, just like that, the years washed away, a collection of sadness and regret massed into a small insular ball of drink and pain.

"I've missed you," Mark suddenly says.

He's not talking to me.

I am lying on the floor in my house, the rain still pounding, the chair broken and askew. My forehead is covered in dry blood. I could tell you this is unusual, but that would be a lie. All that's unusual is the storm and how it will not stop its relentless march across our town. I walk into the bathroom and I wash my face, clean my wound, and bandage it. There are any number of thoughts a man might have at a time like this, but I am most struck by the fact that I am out of alcohol, and that I need to get some more if this storm refuses to abate.

I walk outside, the rain unceasing, the world around me ravaged and furious, a tangled mess of downed power lines and fallen trees. I head to my car, turn it on, and pause to clear my head before heading down the hill to Robby's Liquors. I work my way down, weaving between the branches and abandoned cars, and I'm amazed by just how little my lights are cutting through a darkness that is so opaque as if to be solid, or whole.

But then the darkness breaks, there is light, and with the light I see what the storm has wrought. The water has surged over the banks of the Susquehanna River and buried the South Side in its entirety. MacArthur School is underwater, swollen books floating out of the library windows like pulpy oyster crackers. The cross out front of St. Johns Church is still there too, but just barely, as it rocks to and fro, and threatens to wrench loose at any moment.

Claire and I always talked about us as something that would last until the end of the time.

"When did it stop?" Claire said.

"When did what stop?" I asked, head pounding, shielding my eyes from the morning light.

"Us, that feeling we had, that we were all we needed to be happy, that we would be one until the world stopped spinning," she said dreamily.

"People get older," I said. "Kids leave, things fade with time, and you run out of stuff to talk about. It's normal. What's not normal is being with one person, how could it be?"

"Are you saying you want to be with someone else?" Claire said. "Do you want to see other people?"

"No," I said, cupping her beautiful face, "I'm fine. I was just trying to answer your question."

"I wasn't looking for an answer," Claire said sadly.

Claire and I always talked about us as something that would last until the end of time.

But if this storm marks the end of something, what's the point of keeping anything going?

There is no point, and so here we are.

I continue driving to Robby's and here, closer to the river, everything is completely underwater, and everything is closed. Almost everything. Not Robby's, never Robby's. Even with the rain, the flooding, and the fact that no one with half a brain is even outside, there's Robby's son Robby Jr., just as he is every day, sitting on a milk crate, and holding onto his baseball bat as he guards their parking lot against anyone who might park there without making a purchase.

I park my car and slog through the water towards Robby Jr. The rain is streaming down my face, mixing with the dried blood under the bandage and pooling on my upper lip, the slight tang of copper biting my tongue.

"Hey," Robby Jr. says.

"Hey," I say looking down at him and realizing for the first time that I am barefoot.

"Take what you want," he says, "and leave your money on the counter. My dad went home and we're using the honor system today."

I don't ask him why guarding the parking lot is more important to him than guarding the store. I know why; it's what he knows, and doing anything else but what you know as the world around you warps and melts is too hard to try and grasp.

I take a bottle of tequila and some gin. I also grab some Old Grandad. And two six-packs of Yuengling in case the storm never actually stops. I leave my money on the counter. As I walk by Robby Jr. he taps me on the back with the bat.

"Hey," he says, "you might want to go by Mark's. I know that you know, that he's right off of the riverbank down there, and while I don't suspect you care much about his welfare, I imagine you still care about Claire's."

When I left Thirsty's that night, Claire didn't come with me. She left with Mark and though she came home eventually she kept going back to him. I understood, and it was fine, full circle and all that, but now she hasn't come back at all, and there's this.

Fuck.

I load the alcohol into the car and drive to Mark's house. There are no lights on, but there never are. I walk into the living room which is flooded, as small waves push their way through the front door and out the back again. The smell is rank, and while the rain doesn't help, it's the half-eaten food and dog waste that appears to be the main culprit. I pick my way up the stairs, past the piles of dirty clothes, empty bottles, and abandoned appliances, and they sway and shift with each step. The whole house is dying.

In the bedroom I see them lying on Mark's bed. Both are lightly snoring and half-dressed, the sheets covered in dried vomit. I wrap Claire in a blanket, and I lift her onto my shoulders fireman style, where she bends and morphs, all skin and bones and as light as a child. I pick my way down the sagging stairs and out to my car where I lay her across the back seat. She's unmoving and just as decayed as what's left of our town.

I turn back to stare at the house and I wonder how long it will be before it collapses onto itself and floats away. Because that's how it happens at the end of the world; we disintegrate, we drift, and at some point we are replaced.

Claire moves in the back seat and mumbles Mark's name. I look at her and think that this isn't how we planned it, but nothing ever does go as planned, that's not how it works. With that I head back into the house to get Mark as well. We will face the end of the world together. It only seems fitting.

Stabbed In the Back

I AWAKE TO A SHOOTING PAIN in my lower back, sharp and piercing, and my immediate assumption is that my wife Stephanie is trying to stab me again. When I roll over to face her though, she is not there, and I recall that I am not sure whether she is supposed to be there at all.

I climb out of bed slowly, the pain in my back now paralyzing, and I squeeze my eyes shut as little dots of light bounce across my brain. Stumbling down the hall, the air is moist, the carpet spongy to the touch, and the stink of the flood is still lingering in the walls. I try to focus on one breath, then the next, lips pursed, cheeks sinking in and out, and in again.

Stephanie is sitting on the couch eating a bowl of cereal in the dark, her long hair backlit and shimmering in the moonlight creeping through the blinds, a small ethereal glow emanating from her flawless, nearly translucent skin.

"Hey," she says in her husky voice, the word disappearing in a puff of smoke even as it leaves her mouth.

"Hey," I say, "problem sleeping?"

"Not really," she says smiling.

"No, I suppose not," I say. "Now is that because you're not really supposed to be here? Because I'm thinking that maybe that's what it is."

"Maybe," she says, turning back to her cereal.

A slight clanking sound is emitted each time the spoon hits the side of the bowl. She always hated that sound, but maybe that was before.

"Cool," I say, "I mean not cool, not really, but fine. Anyway, did you try and stab me again?"

"No," she says, "why would you ask that? It was just that one time, and that was like an accident."

"As accidentally as stabbing someone in the back can be," I say, not angrily, though maybe a little nostalgic for what we once had.

"I hope you're not trying to speak in metaphors," she says. "It doesn't suit you."

"No," I say, "I'm just in pain here."

"More metaphor?" she says.

"No, seriously, my lower back is killing me," I respond, "for real."

"For real, cute, let me see," she says.

I look at her. I miss her. I really do, the intimacy, her touch, being in love, all of it.

"Come here," she says.

I smile.

"Not for that," she says, "I can't do that. Just let me get a look at your back."

I walk over and she looks at my back.

"Oh fuck," she says, probing my back, lingering there, her fingers papery and unforgiving.

"What? You're freaking me out," I say.

"I don't know," she says, "it's like a growth, not a bump, more like a nub, it's not soft exactly, but there is activity. You need to get that looked at."

I turn around to look at her, hug her, kiss her, have her tell me it's going to be all right, but she's gone, the house empty, devoid of life and love and anything that used to look like it.

I walk to the doctor's office. I feel the air caress my face and I am scared by the intimacy that even nature can bring.

When was I last outside of the house?

Before the flood certainly, but when was that? And when was the flood exactly? It seems so long ago, and yet there are still tree branches strewn about, and power lines hanging limply from the sky.

There is less pain in my back now, however, though the throbbing is there, lingering, low-grade, just below the surface, and as present as my wife is not.

The doctor is young, skinny, and very pale, too nervous really, but Stephanie found him and I'm not ready to give him up.

"What brings you here today?" he says fidgeting and uncomfortable. "Is it about, well, you know. Do you need someone to talk to?"

"No, that's fine," I say, "she's good."

He grimaces.

"I mean, it's good, it's about my back, I feel like I've been stabbed. Like something is growing there," I say, deciding not to mention my wife again.

"Really, okay," he says, "why don't you stand up and lean over the table."

I lean over the table, lay my face on it, and the cold metal shocks my skin. The doctor lifts my shirt up and runs his fingers over my lower back. They are firm, but light to the touch and pulsing with heat. The hair on my neck stands on end, alive and wiry.

How long has it been since someone touched me like that?

"Yeah," he says, "wow, we don't see this often, but it's what I thought it might be. Take a seat."

I sit. My hand runs to my lower back, the throbbing is more intense, my back is ready to explode.

"What is it," I say, "and can you treat it, what, tell me, please?"

"It's not like that," he says. "It's loneliness."

"I don't understand," I say. "It's a lump, something happened, maybe I was exposed to something when I was cleaning up after the flood, like mold or whatever?"

"No," he says firmly, "it's not about anything that you've come into contact with. It's about what you haven't."

"I'm confused," I say.

"I understand," he says slowly, calmly, speaking more gently now. "Look, you've been exposed to death and decay, the flood, your wife, yet denying all of it, suppressing what's inside you. But it needs to come out. And it will come out. It has to."

"I still don't get it," I say.

"This is about trauma, and fear, and what happens when we can't, or won't, face loss and sadness," he says. "The only recourse is taking these haunted, confusing feelings and exposing them to the world."

"How do I do that?" I say.

"You leave the house," he says, "like you've done today, and you remake a life for yourself, a real life. It's not a cure, but it's the only way."

"Just leave," I say.

"Yes," he says.

"And Stephanie," I say, "what will happen to her?"

"I think you know the answer to that," he says.

So I sit here, back throbbing, Stephanie on the couch reading a book, though intermittently looking at me, not talking, just looking.

I have my shoes on, and I've even packed a bag, but I am hesitating, wondering what I can live with, and ultimately what I cannot.

Barely Breathing

I DON'T WANT TO BE IN THIS CAR, winding through dark, twisty roads in the hills above Two Rivers as the rain is coming down and will not stop. Unceasing, destructive, and taking out everything in its path—trees, power lines, lampposts, and houses, as the water surges above the swollen banks of the Susquehanna River, and flows across the South Side, surging through Thirsty's, across the Plaza 5, the Whole in the Wall restaurant, and Robby's Liquors. And I see all of this because I am stuck in this car I do not want to be in, winding through the dark, flooded streets, with my brother Jack who I don't want to be with either.

Jack who tormented me as a child, the endless globs of spit so very close to my face, dangling there as he pinned me down with this knees.

Jack who drank too much and left home in the middle of the night with a big fuck-you to me, my mom, and dad, no note, no nothing.

Jack who comes and goes, but mostly goes, and who may be a time traveler, for how else to explain his otherwise otherworldly, all-knowing understanding of what is to come?

Jack who knew this storm was coming and that there would be flooding like no one in Two Rivers has seen in a century or more.

How did he know, I don't know, nor do I know where he came from, but there he was on the breezeway, a touch of magic, and the smell of smoke. With his goddamned smile, perfect teeth, cheekbones so sharp they could cut glass, and those funky fucking eyes, one green, and one blue and gold, ethereal, and ephemeral, here, then gone, just like him.

He's back again though, just like that, in the middle of the fucking storm of the century, standing there, with his feathered '80s Scott Baio hair and that goddamn smile, and he grips my shoulder and he says, "We need to go little brother, we have to go to the cemetery and Little John's grave."

Little John, our younger brother, who didn't make it past four months of life, one day full of breath, and the next, not, nothing, just cold.

Our parents never recovered from that, and there they are, inside the house, molded to the couch, unmoving, and barely breathing themselves.

"Do you want to see mom and dad?" I say. "They'll want to see you."

"No, why, who wants that," he says, already moving on in his head.

I do, I want to scream, and I need you to need that. I'm doing this all alone, and I got nothing man, don't you get that?

But he doesn't get that, and he won't, why would he, he's light and space, hurtling across the cosmos, and I am here, nowhere, and lost.

He's just standing in the rain, the fucking rain that will not stop, and we need to go to the cemetery, because he won't do it himself, because that's beneath him. Jack, the fucking boy king of Two Rivers, in his leather jacket, with that hair, and that fucking smile.

But it's not just that either. He knows better than to do this alone. He needs me to be complicit in his crimes. Jack won't go down by himself, he will rise alone, yes, always, but there will be no solo descent.

Even then, there is also the fear of the unknown, and what awaits us, death, and decay, and the idea that someone must be to blame.

He is not without blame, because who is? No one, that's who.

So, we must go to the grave, in this weather, and we have to drive, in my car, though I am not driving. Jack must drive, he is the king, he is back, and this is what we must do, we must be in the car, doing what I don't want to do, on roads I don't want to be on, driving in weather I want to avoid.

"Where have you been Jack," I say, hoping to calm my nerves.

"Everywhere," he says, "from the deserts to the oceans, the future and the past, to Mars and back."

And maybe he has, he's Jack, and who am I to question that?

I suppose I could ask him why Little John's grave is so important to him, but I don't need to. It's not like it's a portal or anything like that, though if it was that might help explain some things.

But no, I know what it is. The money is there, it has to be, the money from the hold-up at the gas station I worked at.

Not that it mattered to him, but I told him too much about how much cash was kept on hand, how Mr. Young would count it at night after the last shift, gleefully, childishly.

How anyone could take it.

Was I showing off? I was. Some messed-up attempt to sound cool, I guess, and did I want something to happen, anything? Maybe I did. Did someone hit me in the back of the head as I swept the front of the station? Under the sickly fluorescent lights, the gnats flying everywhere like a dark cloud hovering overhead. But did I still remain conscious enough to see a leather-jacketed assailant fighting with Mr. Young, as the police sirens started to blare, and that same assailant drive off into the hills, not to be seen since as he traveled from the deserts to the oceans, and maybe Mars? I did. And is that same assailant back now? Coming home for the money he is scared will surface as the rain continues to pound South Mountain and the cemetery begins to flood, and the bodies begin to rise, floating down the mountain and home again?

Because just as the future is the past, the past is destined to repeat itself, the rain will come, the dead will rise, and Jack will get his money.

But we have to get there first, dodging tree branches and downed power lines, as we drive in this car I don't want to be in to somewhere I do not want to go.

Why are animals crossing the road two at a time though? I do not know, but they are, heading up the mountain to whatever something awaits them there.

Which is what we are looking at, Jack and I—cows, porcupines, deer, and pigs trudging along, and we are distracted, and it's raining so fucking hard, and I do not want to be in this car, and there is a thump, and we are spinning, flying, out of control, sliding off of the road and into a ditch, rolling over, the front fender caving in as we go into the side of the ditch with a smash and boom.

Jack isn't wearing his seatbelt and when he flies forward his head hits the window and his chest the steering wheel, and there is blood and slump, as he crumbles into his seat, the car now upside down, stuck, the only sound that of the rain hitting the bottom of the car, which is now the top, as it washes the whole world away.

Jack begins to stir. He is tangled in the steering wheel. Hanging in front of me, and swaying back and forth.

"Get help," he slurs, "I feel this incredible weight on my chest, and I can't move my arms. Do something, please."

I look at him, holding on, and I believe I can do something good here, right, but I don't. Instead, I reach out with my right hand and cover his mouth, and then with my left hand I pinch his nose closed. At first he tries to fight back, wriggling, but then he stops, and he floats away.

There is no more struggle, just the rain, and me, alone, waiting for help, upside down, and free.

God's Work

"WE NEED A TRADITION," Alice says to me, like you can just go and create one whenever you feel like it.

"Who needs a tradition," I say, hoping, praying, she's referring to some other relationship she's part of.

"You and me," Alice says, "we need a thing. The kids are gone and what are we going to do every night? Watch re-runs of *Law & Order* and smoke a joint? Not talking, or even looking at each other as we drift off on the couch? Time is short babe and I don't want that."

This seems like an inappropriate time to tell her how much I have been enjoying our nights, the quiet house, getting high, Sam Waterston's calming timbre and dulcet tones, the last thing we hear before we fall asleep,

"What about sex night?" I say. "Isn't that the grandest of all traditions? A man and a woman, this man and woman, naked as the day they came into the world, sharing fluids and showing their profound love for one another? It's like God's work if you really think about it."

We had installed sex night when the boys were in junior high school. Between practices, rehearsals, counseling, S.A.T. prep, driving lessons, court appearances, rehab, school dances, and on and on, it was so easy to lose ourselves in their lives and forget about ours, what we were, and what we needed.

Frankly, it was the first time in my life I hadn't cared about sex that much. Or more accurately maybe, it was first time I hadn't wanted to expend all of my energy on thinking about sex and trying to get it. When we had it, we had it, and when we didn't, it seemed fine to me.

Sex night was Alice's idea. A friend of hers suggested it. My favorite friend I should add. The idea was if you don't believe you have time, schedule it, value it, and recognize its importance.

Which we did, and as soon as we did, I realized just how much I had missed it, a reminder I suppose, that deciding you don't miss something is not the same as actually missing it.

"Sex night," Alice says, "are you fucking kidding me?"

I look into her deep brown eyes, something I've been doing since I first got lost in them back in high school, and though she may still be speaking, I'm elsewhere, thinking about her breast cancer scare, not even a year before, sitting with her in Two Rivers General, and watching the drip, drip, drip of the chemo trickling into her arm, killing the twisted cells intent on killing her.

At first everyone seemed so old there in the cancer ward, the wispy hair and ashen skin, and they were, but I soon realized that we were old now too, Alice and me, not old old but not young either, and somewhere in the second half of our lives.

"Hey," she said during one especially bad morning when she could not get out of bed, "if I somehow beat this, and then it comes back, I'm not doing all this again, I can't, and I need to know that you're good with that?"

"Yeah," I said lying, wanting every moment with her, every breath and touch.

"You're fucking lying," she said. "You're a terrible fucking liar, it's probably the main reason you never cheated on me, but I'm serious, so look me in the eye and say 'cool,' because I need your blessing, I need to know you get it, and that you're really listening, not that thing you usually do."

"Yeah," I said, "cool."

She had recovered though, and now here we were talking sex, or not, and tradition, though not tradition that involved sex apparently.

"So, why isn't sex night a tradition?" I say.

"Because you have to at least sort of enjoy it," says Alice smiling.

"But I do," I say, "even when you're here with me."

"Touché old friend," Alice says, "but I'm thinking something else, something with meaning and richness, history."

"Oh, you mean like an actual tradition tradition, all right, I see where you're going with this," I say.

I realize now that this whole thing is about mortality, hers and mine, that when the clock begins to feel like it's ticking, really ticking, and time begins to slip away, that's when we start to desperately hold on to what we have.

"So, what are you thinking then," I say, "anything will be fine with me?"

"Not a big deal thing," she says, "but do you remember where we went on our first date?"

I do, like it was yesterday. We had been sophomores in high school. My mother had driven us to Sharkey's where we had met for dinner, City Chicken, shrimp cocktail, fried clams, and a pitcher of Yuengling, because no one carded there, or anywhere back then.

We had stumbled to Alice's house and when we walked into the kitchen her older sister Amy was on the phone, wearing a short nightie that barely covered much of anything at all.

"What the fuck," Alice had screamed at her. "Get out of here."

"Excuse me, what, you little twat," Amy had screamed in return. "Fuck you, get the fuck out of here, and take fucking Clark Kent with you."

No one screamed in my house. We talked civilly. It was fine, but this was electric and I had decided right then that I was marrying into Alice's family by any means necessary.

"Stop thinking about Amy," Alice says, "it's disgusting."

"She was pretty hot," I say. "C'mon, those boobs, wow."

"She's still hot," Alice says.

"Sure she is," I say, "but she's not eighteen anymore."

"Neither am I," Alice says.

This is a trap. You don't talk age, asses, or sisters with your wife, not if you're smart. Which maybe I'm not, having already discussed two of those things, still I haven't touched age yet, and I don't plan to, I've been married long enough to know better than that.

"I was actually thinking about Sharkey's," I say, "so there, why, what were you thinking?"

"That was nicely handled sir," she says, "smooth even. Too bad for you it's not sex night."

"Indeed," I say, "lucky I'm thinking City Chicken though. Hey, do you think that's real chicken?"

"As real as my feelings for you," she says.

"That's my girl," I say reaching for her. "Kiss?"

"Only if you promise to never say it like that again," she says.

"Like what?" I say.

"Like you're seven," she says. "We've done the kid thing and we're done with it."

"Deal," I say.

And with that we kiss.

The day of the new tradition, the rain starts early and never stops. The Susquehanna River starts to swell and then climb above the banks, over the closed bridge, spreading across the streets, coursing through the South Side, flooding basements and businesses alike.

Two Rivers hasn't flooded like this during our lifetime and it hasn't rained like this since biblical times. The smart thing to do is not go out at all, but Sharkey's claims it will be open no matter what, and I don't have the balls to tell Alice I would feel safer staying in, smoking a bowl, and riding it out with Chris Noth and Paul Sorvino.

When we get into the car I can see that the water has climbed up to the fenders of the cars parked in the street as the rain courses down South Mountain only to collect at the bottom of the small hills that serve as our front yards.

I wonder again if I should suggest staying in, the flooded streets, scattered tree branches, and downed power lines as good an argument as any, but then I think about the cancer, *Law & Order*, and old age, and reflect on what it all means. How our time here is limited, how making those we love happy is more important than anything, and that to be scared of a storm, even the storm of the century, seems silly in comparison to trying to live as full a life as possible.

I steer carefully down the driveway, around our floating garbage cans, and onto the street.

There's a moment where I wonder how Alice can be so calm, and I look at her searching for a sign of some kind that she thinks this is stupid too.

Her eyes are closed, so I start to look away, but then stop, caught for a moment in her skin.

Maybe it's the way the sun is setting, refracting through the incessant raindrops and the misty windows, but her skin, her always lovely skin looks different tonight, ashen, and not so much pale, as faded and without life.

It is then that I realize what is happening. She's sick again, very sick, terminal, and this idea of a new tradition, and our going out even on a night like this, is her dying effort to fade away on a happy note.

"What," she says suddenly, her eyes snapping to attention.

"Nothing," I say, "I just love you that's all."

"Oh God," she says, "when did you get like this? And if I promise to put out later, do you promise to stop?"

"Of course," I say, "deal, and done."

"Good," she says. "Now step on it, we don't have forever."

Untrammeled

"IT WAS FUCKING ALIENS, it had to be," Stevey says cowering before me, his forehead glistening in the moonlight, the sweat and rain mixing together and dripping down his face.

I look at him, bat raised, and what I want to say is, "Stevey you are a dick head drunken bastard fuck face cock sucking scamming bastard no good shit tool disloyal scumbag thief who deserves cancer of the balls and syphilitic brain rot that melts your eyeballs until they scab over into puss-ridden postulates filled with taint gunk and sack drippings which render you paralyzed in your sad, lonely house of pain, as the windows crack, the walls crumble, the floor boards warp, and the roof over your sorry ass, rotten cabbage head slowly caves-in, leaving you a blind, crawling sack of shit forced to go place to place, hands out and palms up, begging for crumbs and drink until your knees and elbows crack and blister, slowly wearing away into useless stumps, leaving any further wanderings futile, as you finally find yourself on a sidewalk somewhere, a lumpen mass of hot,

146

disease ridden flesh, and as I come upon you, I will spit on your open wounds and leave you there to decay and become one with an earth that will reject you like a body rejects an organ incompatible with its own survival, because you are death and pestilence, you mother fucking, drunken motherfucker."

But instead, I say, "Aliens, no shit, tell me more."

"It's like a plot," he says. "They created the storm, because they knew the river would swell, the South side would flood, and they could make their move."

"And their play was to abduct you, steal my money and liquor, and then leave it, and you, here at your place you fuck face, lying drunk?" I say.

"I think so," he says, shaking. "Maybe they're trying to sow discord in the streets?"

"The streets of Two Rivers, maybe they were, or maybe you've just got fucking brain damage?" I say, which is probably true anyway the drunken motherfucker.

"I might," he says, "but that doesn't mean I wasn't abducted. It was scary man, the lights and all the medical equipment. The truth is out there bro."

"It is," I say tightening my grip. "Now shut the fuck up motherfucker. Just shut the fuck up."

There is the flood. The storm of the century they say. The Susquehanna River swollen and moaning and splashing over the highway and into the south side of Two Rivers, coursing through the streets, deluging the businesses in its path, and leaving the neighborhood a watery, fetid mess.

It is a good day to stay home. Board up the windows and doors, and pour drink after drink as *The Simpsons* plays on television and the wind outside whips the trees into a frenzied mess. I have a bottle of Scotch and a case of Yuengling and I am ready to ride it out, by myself, feet up, the weather gods half-cocked and skull fucking the skies, while I hunker down, dick in hand, and watch as Homer strangles Bart with his endlessly untrammeled paternal love.

But Robby won't have it.

Robby is batshit crazy and he will guard the parking lot of the liquor store from non-paying customers at all costs, and in any weather.

"What kind of man lets someone park in his lot without making a purchase?" Robby always says. "I'll tell you, the same kind of man who watches another man fuck his wife. And that kind of man is no man at all."

Who can argue with that?

I can't, but I'm Robby's son, and what kind of man argues with this father? Not this one.

The whole time I was growing up, Robby sat out by the parking lot of our liquor store like the Buddha, Zen and tranquil, and merging with his natural surroundings. This assuming of course that the Buddha spent his time on earth resting a baseball bat across his polyester pants waiting for someone to take a spot in his parking lot, but not buy any liquor from his store.

Which is possible, I don't know much about the Buddha.

I do know that Robby had me wait on customers until I was old enough to sit in the parking lot myself, which I have done, bat in lap, day after day, and through all kinds of weather ever since.

Until now anyway, because now there are floods, and Arks being built, and I tell Robby no, no way, no one, not even him, or the Buddha himself, can work the parking lot in this weather.

"What kind of man lets someone park in his lot without making a purchase?" Robby says. "I'll tell you, the same kind of man who watches another man fuck his wife. And that kind of man is no man at all."

"Truth," I say, not wanting to argue. "But there aren't going to be any customers either."

"It doesn't matter," Robby says. "We are open 365 days per year, we will open today, and you will guard the motherfucking lot."

Some part of me knows this is about trying to control what can be controlled when nothing seems all that controllable in the first place. But the larger part of me isn't listening. I am floating somewhere outside of the conversation, and thinking about the one summer Robby had let me go to camp.

We had gone on a canoe trip on the Susquehanna, and at one point the current slowed to a turgid morass of water and silt, and we put up our feet and just floated. It is the closest I've ever come to bliss, and freedom, and I have wanted to experience that feeling again ever since.

I will not be experiencing it today however.

I take up my spot in the parking lot, bat in lap, and I am soaked to the bone from the start. It turns out that customers do come and go, having made the decision to eschew food for drink and riding out the day. Too wet to stand, and too cold to truly care, I leave the door open and let them pay by the honor system, leaving the correct amount of the counter.

And then that squirrel fuck Stevey pulls up in his truck.

His once beautiful skin is as pale and mottled as always, though with the rain he's even more washed-out than usual, ghostly and translucent. His hand are shaking, which might be related to the temperature, though it's just as likely the result of too little alcohol, his brain slowly drying out, even as the rest of the world becomes saturated and the consistency of soaked bread.

"Hey, Robby Jr.," Stevey says. "I'm glad I found you. It's an emergency."

I know the pitch for free liquor will come next.

"Yeah, I know," I say. "There's a storm, and flooding, the world has gone to shit, and you have no alcohol, and no money. I got it. Thanks for the update man."

"No dude, I just went by your house," he says all shaky and weird, "and your dad fell down. He hit his head or some such shit. I think he's dying."

A wave of terror passes over me and possibly some relief, but mostly terror. I try to calm myself by thinking about being out on the river, and how everything in the world is still possible for me.

"You left him there?" I ask.

"Yeah, I was scared," Stevey says. "You know your dad. I thought he was going to yell at me."

I don't even bother to reply, I just start running, bat in hand, the flood waters splashing around my ankles with every step. I don't stop until I get home and I can't breathe any more.

I open the door.

"What the fuck are you doing here," Robby screams, "and who's watching the fucking parking lot?"

Fuck me.

I run out of the house and back through the flood waters to the store. When I walk in I look around. All the money is gone, and shelves of alcohol are missing as well, including every bottle of vodka, Stevey's favorite.

I walk to Stevey's house. I try to think about that river again, but it's impossible, it's lost to me. I tighten my grip on the bat and when I get to Stevey's house I see him lying there on the living room floor surrounded by wet dollar bills and empty vodka bottles.

He's half awake.

I raise the bat above my head, drops of rain dripping onto my face, and Stevey stirs.

"It was fucking aliens, it had to be," Stevey says.

The Runner

"WHAT THE FUCK," Landry says to no one in particular on the first day of high school track practice. "Is he going to be like this all the time?"

Landry with his feathered hair and pigeon-toed strides is the golden boy miler and undisputed leader. I hate Landry already and I know that will never change; when hate takes hold, you have to learn how to live with it. If not it corrodes and so do you.

I also love him, though, which is the way it is with people who are so much cooler than you are.

There is also Landry's sidekick, Donnie, ramrod straight, eyes forward, one step behind Landry, always; and Ron, my sort of friend from the neighborhood, with his wispy mustache, slight frame, and eager-to-please countenance.

"No, Landry, he's cool," Ron says, pleading. "Seriously, and he's going to buy some real running shoes—right, Lee?"

I'm running in my canvas Nike tennis shoes. I don't know about running heel-to-toe or anything else. I just know that running makes me feel alive and indestructible as I slap the road with every step, the sound echoing across South Mountain where we keep silently and rhythmically climbing as the sun sets, the sweat settles in a light film on our backs, and the sky stretches across our home town of Two Rivers like a shadow.

"Yeah," I say quietly. "I'm getting new shoes."

"Good," Landry says. "Now shut the fuck up. This is a sacred space, and we are gods."

Landry may or may not be a god, but we treat him as such; we have to.

This is in part because he is a miler and there is nothing more glamorous than that. It is also the hair and the dazzling white teeth, neither of which anyone of us knows how to obtain, and his facility with women—even the mere fact that he will talk to them at all is mesmerizing for us. Ultimately though, it is his fierce competitiveness that most holds us in his thrall. He is not scared to compete: every race is seen as something to be deconstructed, owned, and controlled. For him, to race is to live, to win is glorious, and we fear doing anything that will get in the way of this, or him.

So maybe we are not gods, but he just might be.

Of course, to be a god is to be flawed, and to think you can control anything is to eventually control nothing at all. And so it is with Landry, no sense that rivals can emerge, no sense that they might even exist.

There we are at a dual meet, though not even an important one, some lame-ass high school and us, when Donnie somehow beats Landry in a race. Landry doesn't say anything. He just walks away. Just like that. This doesn't seem like Landry, and it isn't.

"It's not loaded," Landry says the next night as we sit in his car after practice and he pulls out a gun. "Here, check it out."

I don't want to check it out.

"Take it," he says, semi-smiling, semi-not.

I take it.

"I want you to wave it around Donnie," Landry says. "In private, and then tell him that you think him winning that race was not cool, not fucking cool at all."

"It was one race," I say, taking the gun and feeling its heft as I pass it from hand to hand and then lift it into the air and point it towards the setting sun.

"That doesn't matter," Landry says.

"I don't want to," I say. "This is stupid."

"You're a pussy, bro," he says reaching for the gun.

I hate him for being weak and flawed, and for being human, and hating Landry for these things is so much worse than hating him for being superhuman.

If he is just like the rest of us, what are we?

We are nothing.

He grabs the barrel, and I pull back, not ready to give it up, and not ready to give into him. It goes off. Just like that. And Landry's dead, slumped over the steering wheel, not moving, no nothing really, except for a little trickle of blood working its way down the side of his face.

There is a moment when I feel a sense of relief and freedom, but it's quickly replaced by fear and regret and the sense that I should just run off into the woods, no pause and no explanation. No one would question that. But I don't, I can't, and so I pause, and soon people are running towards the car, and my path is set for me.

No one asks what happened—later they will, but outside of the police, no one ever asks directly. The gun belongs to Landry's dad Frank and it was an accident, it had to be.

That is enough to explain it.

Well, that and the belief that sometimes you cannot explain these things. There are no reasons, and no true solace.

There is no punishment either except for the punishment I subject myself to.

Because that moment, the gun firing, the sound of it echoing in that enclosed space, the shattering of eardrums and lives, that does not fade, not ever. I cannot sleep. I cannot look people in the eyes. It's all too much. The memories following me across the years, the guilt, and the constant smell of gunpowder that never quite goes away. Even the smallest noises resonate in my head as gunfire.

So I run, always, measuring steps, counting miles, punishing myself with this solitary pursuit, as I try to outpace the shadows ever creeping across my bruised mind. Out there, on the road and trails, where there is no anger, no sadness, just one step after another. And so it goes, day after day, month after month, then years, until tonight.

There is a storm, the storm of the century they're calling it. People are encouraged to stay inside and avoid the constant rat-tat-tat of the rain, the downed power lines, the fallen trees. But I can't stay in, and I won't, and my heart is pounding at the mere thought of it.

I lace up my shoes and head into the hills, through the woods, the lightning crashing like bowling pins all around me. The air is electric and I am aglow, like a god, a fallen god rising from the ashes.

I head onto the road that bisects South Mountain, arms pumping, jaw loose, and eyes nearly closed by the incessant rain hitting me in the face.

There is a moment, where the lightning and the crashing and everything around me threatens to take me back to Landry's car, but I am distracted by a couple of bears ambling across the road, and I am struck by the fact that they are glowing, bathed in the ethereal light that emanates through the storm clouds overhead.

I slow down to take in the majestic sight before me and see that there is a car overturned in a ditch by the side of the road that is slowly filling with water. There are two men inside, one lying peacefully across the steering wheel, the other banging on the window.

My inclination is to keep running. No contact, no emotion, no pain. But I pause, and after that my path is clear, and it is one of my choosing.

I climb down the embankment and wade into the chest-high, murky water, the rain continuing to pound my head. I lean towards the window, cup my mouth with my hands and shout, "I have to wait until the car is totally submerged."

The sound of my voice is startling to me, covered with dust from lack of use, and sounding like someone else's completely. Someone I don't know, someone not me.

When the car is fully submerged, I remove my top layer, wrap it around my fist and punch the window until it breaks. As the water surges into the car, I unhook the man's seatbelt and he floats out to me, like a baby, bloated now, and unconscious.

I drag him to the road and begin CPR, then mouth to mouth.

How long has it been since I touched someone else?

He starts to cough, then breathe, rolling over and spewing out the buckets of water previously sitting in his throat and lungs.

When his eyes go wide, and his life has returned to him, I shake the glass out of my top, put it back on, and run off into the night.

Watching and Waiting

"I'M GOING OUT to see if I can help," he said.

"Fine," you said.

What else was there to say? Please don't go out in this weather? Don't leave me alone, while I sit here cowering in the dark, too scared to move or even breathe?

You weren't raised like that, but he wouldn't have listened anyway. He never did, which at first had been part of the attraction. You could have him, but you couldn't push him to do anything he didn't want to do.

"I want you to put some bushes out in front of the house," you said.

You had hired him to do some landscaping.

"Why?" he asked.

"I want to block the windows," you said. "I want more privacy."

"You don't know what you want," he said, "and I won't do that for you. You need to see the world, not hide from it. That's how things work, or should anyway."

You don't know if he was right, but he didn't plant the bushes regardless. He also never left, and you loved that, the idea that someone can come into your life when you are past thinking it is even a possibility. Here you are now though, sitting by the window, day after day, like some sea captain's wife, healing, looking, and waiting for something to happen.

It is after the flood and the world didn't end as predicted. It may not have even been the storm of the century. Still, damage was done, there is always damage. Downed power lines, uprooted trees, homes and businesses underwater, the memories built there floating in the half light, ghostly and beckoning.

The workmen are out there now, picking up branches, running them through the wood chipper, the endless grind and whir echoing throughout the neighborhood, and bouncing off of the surrounding mountains, only to nestle uneasily in your brain. The men are indistinguishable for the most part, hard hats and tight jeans, flannel shirts, and safety vests. They are unshaven and cliché in the way small towns always are.

Things may be destroyed, the past drowned and forgotten, and time may fitfully march on as it always does, but nothing ever really quite changes. Thirsty's still serves beer, the Susquehanna River still flows, and you are here by the window, watching, waiting, wondering how you got here at all. Not leaving home, you get that, you never liked to leave home, but to be alone again, and unable to bear the isolation, that's different, new. Before you had a taste of companionship you didn't even know you wanted it, but now that it's gone, you need more of it to make this feeling stop.

It would help if one of the workmen would come to your door again. Though not just any of the workmen, because they're not all indistinguishable are they? No, there is one that's distinct. There is the crooked nose, and the hair on his knuckles, thick and alive. You saw it the one time he came to the door and asked to use the phone. He was so polite, quick, didn't linger, but you wouldn't have minded if he had. Just as you wouldn't have minded him holding you, and asking how you were doing, commenting on how it must be hard to be alone.

"What's your story?" he might have said.

"Nothing," you would have said, "nothing interesting, I hurt my back during the flood, I was trying to barricade the doors and windows, and it was too much, too much lifting, too much stress. I ended up falling on the floor, I rode it out, and now I've barely moved since."

You might wonder if you've said too much, sharing more information than he could handle, or care about it, but you've been alone, there's no one to check on you, and no buffer, plus he seems so kind.

"You had no one to help you," he might have said, looking concerned, confused too, but definitely concerned.

"No," you would have replied, "my husband went out to help down at the river when the rain started, and then he never came back."

"I'm sorry for your loss," he would have said.

"Thank you," you would have answered, not telling him that it's not that your husband died, he just didn't come back. How you know he left and didn't just get swept away by the flood, you can't say for sure, you just know. But you wouldn't have said any of that anyway, and he wouldn't have held you regardless, as much you would have wanted that. Instead, he would have just left, unsure how to continue, still polite, but gone, back to his crew, and away from your neediness and desperation.

He probably doesn't even know what loneliness looks like.

How the days start to pile up on one another, weighing you down, becoming oppressive and unwieldy.

He has his work crew, who you imagine he drinks with after work, and plays softball with once a week. They never win, but no one cares, it's another excuse to ignore the bills and spouses. At home he has family, or he did, he's divorced, and you can see it all so clearly. Because now that he legally has to spend time with his kids, he does so more than he ever did before. It's only two nights a week and every other weekend, but when they're together, they're really together for the first time, working on homework, going bowling at Laurel Bowl, attending little league games, and running out for Speidies at Lupos. There are even family dinners every so often, something they barely did at the end, but he and his ex are fine, and so much better than they ever were as an actual couple. Then there's his girlfriend, younger, but not much, never married, no interest in kids, always preferred working for her father at his law firm, drinking, and adventure, white water rafting, and hunting. Their weekends are full of fucking, at least when the kids aren't there, and the only breaks they take are for water, and watching episodes of *Breaking Bad*.

He has a whole life, and that's important to recognize, because if he's never alone, and if he's never really been alone, he can't know what it's like to feel like you do, and if anything, what you have might seem like a relief to him from the outside, a break from family, work, expectations, and responsibilities.

You never wanted those things, but things are different now, and how can you share any of this with a stranger? You can't, you won't, so you sit here, day after day, watching the men clear the trees, and knowing they'll be done soon.

After that you don't know what you'll do, but you're not planning that far ahead.

You think about him, your husband, taking this moment to

make a clean break and start anew, somewhere far away from here. He has a new life, and maybe even a new identity. He can be anything and anyone he wants to be, and you wonder what he says about himself, that his wife is dead, that he lost his job, or that he's always wandered, but now wants to put down some roots?

You don't really know, but that's because you don't know much about his secret life, the parts he kept from you, the parts we all keep from one another in relationships, the dreams and the hopes. But he's acting on them now, he must be, he better be.

What about you though, what do you want, and why are you still here, when what once seemed fine, doable, all seems so empty now?

There is your back, but that will pass, and the workman's knuckles, though your feelings about that will pass too. This is your home, and that means something in a world so potentially fraught with imminent disaster and pain. Stability is good, safe, and to be anchored is to know your place in the world. There is value in that.

Not that there was value in that for your husband, not after the flood came. Though maybe there never was, because maybe it's not true that you didn't know about his secret life and dreams, maybe you just chose to ignore them?

You think back to the night the two of you were lying out back in the hammock behind the house, and staring at the helix of stars that seemingly went on forever.

"If you could live anywhere in the world," he said, "where would that be?"

"Is this real?" you said.

"What do you mean?" he said.

"Like do I really plan to live there," you said. "That's what I mean, because if it's real, than nowhere, this is home."

"You can't even pretend can you?" he said.

"No, that's never worked for me, my parents always said there was no use wanting what you can't have," you said, running your hands along his thigh.

"Why can't you have it," he said. "Aren't you only limited by your imagination?"

You knew you couldn't answer that, because you couldn't imagine anything else for yourself. You wished he just understood that, or that you could say that to him, but how do you say that and not sound impossibly lacking? You can't. So you didn't.

"What about you," you said moving the focus off of yourself. "Where could you picture living?"

You want him to say nowhere. That he prefers to be anywhere you are.

"Everywhere," he said dreamily. "I want to live everywhere."

You looked at him and he was staring off into the stars, already lost to you. You kissed him hard on the mouth, the neck, his stomach, each kiss an effort to make him forget every place in his head that could possibly take him away from you.

You realize now that he tried to be something for you that he could not be. And maybe he tried really hard to do so, and maybe he did not, but you decide to believe it was real anyway. That there had been feelings, and desire, and when it became all too oppressive and limiting, he had to go, because what other choice did he have?

You don't recognize how lost you are in your thoughts until the moment the air explodes through your window, the piercing screech, the black mass of noise and flutter, engulfing you, and speeding around the front room, sowing chaos with every passing moment. You bring your hands up to your head, you cover your eyes, and you scream as you tumble from your chair and fall onto the floor, the jarring pain in your back mashing into the fear of the unknown now crashing into your brain.

It grows quiet just as suddenly as it grew fierce, the chaos becomes calm, and you look up from your place on the floor, carefully trying to assess what has entered your home and head, and whether whatever it is is even real.

As you look up you see it; a raven is sitting on the bookshelf, it's breathing hard, and staring at you with its piercing, black eyes. Your mother always told you that ravens are visitors from the other side, and that they come when you need a reminder that those you lost are watching over you and that things will be okay. Your mother never left the house though.

You start to cry, first quietly then more excessively, hugging yourself as you lose your breath, the pain in your back hugging you back and refusing to let go. The tears quickly turn into laughs, somewhat crazy, but hearty and full as well, and as you try to collect yourself, you look up again and he is standing there, the man with the knuckles.

"Are you okay?" he asks.

Freddie's Dead

Freddie went and hugged the flood.
Freddie floundered in the mud.
Freddie went crazy in the head.
And now Freddie Flounder is dead, dead, dead.

THIS IS THE SONG we drunkenly sang after the flood and after Freddie Flounder was dead, and no longer around for us to mock and tease.

He wasn't there anymore for us to pour milk in his locker or clap his ears with our hands when we sat behind him on the bus.

We couldn't call him fag or snap his alabaster ass in the locker room with our towels. We would never follow him down the street threatening to rape his sister or set his house on fire.

No one would be able to call his home to let his mother know that his father had died in a car crash on the way home from work, was being accused of molesting children, or had left her for another man because she was such a fucking whore.

He was no longer there for us to plan his imminent demise as we took long bong hits at parties in the endlessly empty houses where our parents were not around, and would not be around, until some magical time when they sobered up, cut down on business travel, or merely came home from whatever secret debaucheries they engaged in when we had no idea where they were or what they were doing.

Did we care that they were not around?

We did not.

Did we think our behavior was wrong, or feel anything approaching empathy for fucking Freddie Flounder that pale-faced fuck, and the torment he endured?

Not at all.

He deserved it. He had earned it. And not just by the mere dint of his birth or presence, and the unfortunate twist of fate where someone is chosen to be bullied because they arrive fully deformed with a target on their back.

No, fucking Freddie Flounder had earned our ire.

Now was it true that no one would quite remember what he had done to earn it?

It was.

It might have been the time he let his clothes fall out of his locker in gym class and his underwear clearly had shit in it. Not that we were definitely sure they were his clothes.

Or maybe it was that time he tried to talk about jerking-off in homeroom. Who does that? Well, who talks about it anyway? No one, and it's possible he wasn't really trying to talk about masturbation? Maybe we misunderstood what he was saying, but what the fuck Freddie fucking Flounder?

It could have been because of his pale, nearly translucent skin, the subtle swish in his walk that we were all sure we saw, the fact that he never wanted to look for tit during movies on HBO, or how he talked to our mothers at sleepovers, our fucking mothers, once telling one that he wondered what it was like to get pregnant? Assuming that last part was true, because were our mothers around for sleepovers? And did Freddie Flounder ever actually come to one?

It didn't matter, but it definitely could have been any of that, even if no one could totally swear any of it was technically true.

What we were sure of though, is that one summer at the pool when we were all jammed together in the changing room, talking about all of the pussy we had never seen, but would, Freddie Flounder popped a chubby, right there for everyone to see.

A chubby, fuck no, Freddie Flounder.

Fuck yes, and sure, he tried to cover it up, but he wasn't fast enough. It was impossible, and the damage was done.

When rain came to Two Rivers, they said it might be the storm of the century. The Susquehanna River rose so high that it sloshed over the highway, something no one could ever remember happening before. Power lines were downed, trees felled, and even the parking lot at Robby's Liquor Store was under water. We were all told to stay in, lay low, and ride it out.

Which was fine with us, no school, yo, awesome. So we hung out in our empty houses, the windows boarded up, and we drank our Yuengling and smoked our bowls, until our heads throbbed in a sloppy, Jell-O mess; our lips burned, all tingly and chapped at the edges; and we found ourselves nodding off, stuporous and fucking stupid.

Everyone that is, but Freddie Flounder.

His windows were boarded up too. And his parents knew what everyone else knew. They were even home playing cribbage or some such shit.

But Freddie Flounder still got outside.

He walked down his front walk, dodging power lines and branches, bracing against the wind, and then he waded into the ever-climbing flood waters.

As he walked along, he gathered stones, and he crammed them into his pockets until they began to bulge, and the water started rising up to his waist and beyond.

I wonder what he was thinking then and whether he was scared, knowing that soon the water would rise to his chest, creeping up his neck and over his mouth, his nostrils still uncovered, as the air became more and more limited, and he began fighting to breathe.

That's assuming Freddie fought at all.

Maybe he was resigned to this fate at that point, embracing his choice, thinking that the freedom that awaited him was far preferable to anything that would come after the flood.

Was there a moment though where he questioned his decision? Did he stop to consider that maybe there wasn't a different path? That this was in fact a temporary solution, and that things get better?

I hope he did.

But I also hope that he didn't suffer much, that he wasn't battered as he was pulled under the water and all those tree branches coursed and bounced along with him.

And I really hope that he wasn't too scared, because the idea that he might have lingered, trapped in the blanket of water around him for anything longer than it took to feel the freedom he sought is unbearable to me.

Later, much later, and way after the flood, when we saw each other at reunions, weddings, and on work trips, no one could quite remember when the incident at the pool actually happened. Or if it was even at the pool, maybe it was actually the ice rink? But if it was the ice rink, why would Freddie Flounder have been changing?

That didn't make sense. Nor could anyone even really remember who was there when it happened. Maybe it was someone's older brother? Maybe that's how we knew about it? Or maybe it was someone else entirely, and not Freddie Flounder at all?

No one was totally sure anymore, but that didn't matter by then, Freddie Flounder was dead and he had taken the answers to these questions with him to his watery grave.

Vision

"WHAT ARE YOU BUILDING?" Joe at the lumber yard asks me, the slight sign of a smirk crossing his face, his crazy eyes looking as crazy as ever.

We both know that I fucked his wife Stacey in high school, and they apparently have a running debate about whether she left him at the time for the sole purpose of doing so, or he left her because he was tired of hearing her talk about me.

Regardless, we fucked at a party. She was drunk and laughing and bent over a small fence in the backyard of the house we were at, her summer dress floating there in the night air, her head bouncing with every thrust.

When we finished, we both smiled, she walked back into Joe's arms, and that was mostly that.

Now they are married, we occasionally drink together at Thirsty's, and when Stacey is really drunk, she likes to talk about that night. It's a game we play.

"You were the last one I was with before Joe and I went and got married," Stacey will say. "What do you remember?"

"That you were a vision," I say, "and that I compare everyone I've been with since to you."

This makes her smile, which makes me happy. Joe too apparently.

"Pete, man," he once said to me all serious, "whatever it is you and Stacey talk about back there in the bar, please keep doing it. Those nights are crazy. Last time you guys hung out, I ended up doing her in our backyard bent over the fence. Awesome, right?"

I suppose so, and it's not that I'm lying when I tell her she was a vision or that I compare everyone to her. She was a vision with her creamy skin and flowing blonde hair. And I have compared everyone to her since then.

That night, that fuck, is preserved in amber, like a fossil, or a time capsule, a perfect little memory where everything else falls short. Every fuck, every woman, every relationship, they all pale in comparison, and they have to, they are real, and that, that isn't, not anymore.

"Hey man, seriously, what's the wood for," Joe says, "and do you think you might want to get some drinks with us tomorrow night? Stacey and I are planning to go out and I'm sure Stacey would be happy to see you."

"I don't know brother," I say. "You know I'm happy to take care of you and all, but I need to work on this thing."

"Think about it," he says grinning. "Please."

"Of course," I say, before taking my wood and throwing it in the back of my truck.

From there I head out to the cemetery where my dad is buried. It's peaceful here with its sloping hills and trees, the endless skies, and the view of the river off past the woods and across the way. On a quiet day you can even hear the water sloshing up on shore, which is nice for when I sleep here, which is often. I don't know when it started. At first, it was a place I came to drink and hang out, and acknowledge that I wasn't going to escape my father's long, drunken shadow any time soon.

But at some point, being here just seemed better than being anywhere else. Things didn't make sense in other places. They never did, but it's worse now. Now that I can't blame my anger or confusion on his sickly, ghost-like presence. It's just me and the life I didn't make and don't have, and who needs that?

I place an open can of Yuengling on the grass, I lay the two-by-fours down by the grave, side by side, and I start to drill. I am building a platform with a small roof, a place to sleep, and maybe keep a cooler, a generator, a mattress, and a lamp. I can get away with this because no one really comes here, it's a dying town, and though my dad liked to joke that the cemetery was the only place everyone was dying to get into, even that's not true anymore. Everyone is dying to get out; well, everyone but me, and Joe and Stacey maybe.

I drift off, hammer in hand, empty cans and nails scattered everywhere, my work half-done at best. I awake at dawn to the plink, plink, plink of rain on my face at first light, and then stronger. I pop a beer and get back to work, drill, hammer, repeat, my platform slowly expanding from something the size of a man to something more akin to a small deck.

The rain keeps coming down. It's pouring now, and it's almost impossible to see anything more than a few inches away from my face.

I climb into the truck to dry off and as I look out of the window I see for the first time how high the river is, the water swirling and roiling, and begging to pour onto the shore and beyond.

When I turn on the radio they say it is the storm of the century, that there is no end in sight, and that residents are being encouraged to stay inside of their homes, ride it out, and as is their want, pray to whatever higher power they may ascribe to.

I pop open another beer and get back to work.

As I kneel there, the hammer slipping with every strike of a nail, two deer, a buck and a doe, walk out of the woods on the outskirts of the cemetery. They are followed by two skunks, and then a pair of raccoons, all of whom dutifully line up a small distance from the platform. I don't make eye contact with them, or even treat their presence as anything but normal. Instead I continue working in this manner even as two brown bears sidle up to the others, and a pair of geese take residence on their backs.

The rain keeps coming, I keep working, and when I finally look at my watch I see that the whole day has passed. I realize that I am getting very low on wood and that the lumber yard will be closing soon. I then think about Joe and Stacey, who will be getting drinks storm or no storm, and briefly lose myself in how lovely Stacey is, her kindness and still creamy skin merging into something more than the woman I've been flirting with since high school. Something earthier, more regal, and after all these years, one of the few people I know how to spend time with at all.

I shake my head like an Etch-A-Sketch to make her image go away, I wave goodbye to the animals who nod accordingly, and I head down to the lumber yard where Joe is closing up.

"Hey man," he says, his crazy eyes popping, "what are you doing out in this weather? This is like end of the world shit."

"I was working on that thing," I say, "and I'm starting to think that I'm going to need more wood, a lot of it."

"Yeah, well we're closing brother, maybe when the storm lets up," he says.

"Yeah, well it's not going to let up, so what if I promise to join you guys tonight. Can I get some wood then?" I reply.

"Take all the wood you need," he says.

I load up the truck and then I drive over to Thirsty's where I drink with Joe and Stacey and anyone else who ambles by.

At some point Stacey and I steal our way to the back of the bar.

"You were the last one I was with before Joe and I went and got married," Stacey says, "What do you remember?"

"That you were a vision," I say, "and that I compare everyone I've been with since to you."

She smiles.

"Hey," I say, "are you happy?"

"What," she says. "Why would you ask me something fucked-up like that?"

I realize that I have messed with the order of the way things are, have been, and are supposed to remain, but if this rain is going to continue, and the end of the world is upon us, maybe it's time to throw caution to the wind.

"I want you to meet me tomorrow morning at the cemetery," I say. "I want you to join me for something."

"In this weather, no, I don't know, maybe, why not," she says.

"Good," I say, "take care of what you need to tonight and then come up first thing, okay?"

"Okay," she says.

I get back into my truck and I drive through the flooded streets, past the downed power lines and trees, the river now crashing over the riverbank, as it courses through town.

When I get back to the cemetery, I see that two garter snakes, a pair of chipmunks, and a couple of horses have joined the menagerie, all standing there stoically despite the storm, and the wind buffeting them from all sides.

I start to work again, and the animals keep coming, cows, possums, dogs, and cats. By morning the water from the river is slowly climbing up the hill and towards the cemetery, still far enough away to not yet be a concern, but close enough that time is escaping us with every drop of rain.

Stacey pulls up in her car and looks at me spellbound.

"Is that what I think it is?" she says stepping out of her car.

"It is," I say, "and you are a vision. Are you ready to come with me on a journey?"

"Why not," she says.

With that, Stacey joins me on the platform, where is she followed by the animals, two by two, the world now underwater, the rain unceasing, and the possibilities endless.

What We Talk About When We Talk About the Flood

IT IS BILL, Jenna, Holly, and me and we are talking about love.

Actually, that's not entirely accurate, what we are talking about is the flood. They say it is the storm of the century, and who are we to argue, especially when we're talking about love, and have more important things to argue about anyway.

"Are we out of gin?" Holly says, lifting the gin bottle in front of her, turning it upside down, and shaking it. Holly is my second wife. Not that we are married, it's just that we might as well be.

Holly has these long, red ringlets of hair, it's like fire, and she had been my receptionist, but I would go home at night after work, and all I could think about was seeing her hair draped across my pillow in the morning.

My ex-wife's hair was fine, black as night and nearly translucent, but it didn't look like fire, and that wasn't going to work.

Plus, she didn't drink.

Her father had been a drunk, and terrible to her mother, before he went and died in a pool of blood right in front of them one night at the kitchen table after a coughing attack gone terribly wrong.

No one could save him, so she married a doctor, me, because I could save things, just not our marriage.

Holly drinks, and between that and the fire and the pillowcase, well that was that.

"No gin, no biggie," Jenna says, "nothing wrong with vodka."

Jenna is a blonde. She's a student of Bill's and she's not much to look at frankly. She has a pug nose, and her eyes are too close together. But she's young, goddamn it, and she's fresh, and that's not nothing. She seems so new, and new isn't always better, but then you brush against her skin, and it's fucking electric, and there's nothing wrong with that.

There is something wrong with vodka, however, it's not gin, hence the arguing and our going around in circles.

"There's gin," I reply. "There's always gin."

I can drive to Robby's Liquor Store if I have to, they'll be open during the storm, but I shouldn't drive, I shouldn't even walk.

Of course by that standard, the not being safe standard, we should be ensconced in the house, the windows boarded up, and listening to the rat-rat-rat of the rain on the roof as we drink our gin and talk about love.

But we're not.

We're sitting in the backyard around the picnic table, drinking as the flood waters rise, the power lines twitch and fall, and tree branches start to float by, passing through our backyard and into the next one.

We could go inside, but we could do many things, talk to our estranged children, visit our parents' graves, or even sober up, but if this truly is the end of world, why would we want to do so?

No reason.

"Let's go look for the gin," Bill says pulling on my arm.

Where did all of this start?

Thirsty's probably, an afternoon drink stretching into an evening one, a weekly rip becoming daily, and soon no one is anywhere, but here, around the table, drinking gin, and talking about love.

Bill and I dig through the cabinets above the sink.

"I'm thinking of asking Jenna to marry me," Bill says. "What do you think about that?"

What do I think? I think he's been married five times already, all students of his, all young and enthralled with a onetime wunderkind best-selling author turned small-town professor, turned functioning alcoholic. But what do I say?

"I think it's grand," I say, clapping him on the back as I find the last bottle of gin.

We walk back out to Holly and Jenna, the flood waters now pooling around their ankles, their dresses saturated up to their calves, both of them laughing and struggling to hold the table in place.

I raise the bottle triumphantly over my head like a trophy.

Holly and Jenna start to cheer.

Bill and I sit down at the table, our pant legs soaked, the water now knee high, small waves coursing through the backyard.

"To love," I shout over the storm as I pour everyone a drink.

"To love," they all shout back lifting their glasses to the lips.

And then we drink to love as the rain plasters our hair to our foreheads, the flood waters rise, and we slowly float away.

We Were All Here

THERE WAS MY WIFE LILLY, a writer, with her long black curls and crazy, angled cheekbones. She was from Chicago and favored wrap sweaters that accentuated her not-so-bountiful cleavage.

There was Bob, he of the big, gap-toothed smile and awful crewcut. He was a banker and liked to eat Kobe beef burgers on his company expense account.

Kelly was a blonde from Texas who had inexplicably come to Two Rivers to be something other than the former cheerleader, soon to be the trophy wife she was raised to be.

Frank was a lobbyist. He had grown up in a small town nearby. He was so good-looking, with his chiseled jaw and good hair, and so charismatic on top of that, the town couldn't contain him.

Bonnie was a red-haired marketing chick who spent all day ensuring that people *Got Milk*. She talked so much at work she barely said a word the rest of the time.

And then there was me, Jeff, an actuary with thinning, coarse hair and issues—according to Lilly anyway—with aggression, passive and otherwise.

We were all here together, in Two Rivers, standing around the island in Frank and Bonnie's kitchen, the storm of the century upon us.

Everyone was smiling, bantering, the kids running around the house, yelling, crazy, laughing, being kids and now old enough to entertain themselves, so we could actually stand there and have some drinks, and talk, actually talk.

Not that Bonnie talked. She said this was because she talked all day at work, pitching and hustling. But we also knew this was because of Frank and his endless need to take over every room, fill it up and suck the air out of it until it all belonged to him. And people loved him for it, on the golf course and in Albany where he held court like a young prince.

We loved him too, in the way you love attractive people and are hoping, that by loving them, some of their beauty will rub off on you. Still, we were all here for Bonnie, and if, or more accurately when, they divorced we all knew she was welcome to claim us as part of her haul.

The question for me was whether I had a shot at Bonnie. Now, did this mean I wanted to cheat on Lilly? No. Not consciously. But did I wonder what it might be like, I did, just like I wondered if Lilly would sleep with Frank if she could, assuming she hadn't already.

Did I really know what she was up to all day while I was at work and she claimed to be writing? Further, were you really a writer if you had never actually published anything? Well, besides some early pedestrian stuff in student literary magazines?

Isn't art in the transaction? This wasn't clear to me, but did it even matter, no, not tonight, not when we were trying to ignore the storm, having so much fun, and the kids were running around, and away, from us, full of joy and frolic.

Still, we did have questions about Kelly and Bob. Kelly's husband Jason had fucked the preschool teacher. We all wanted to, if just so we could hear her yell our names in her thick, Serbian accent. Kelly had not been so understanding and now Jason was out of the picture because Lilly and Bonnie had decided he was out, and Frank and I had decided we weren't going to fight with them.

We really liked Jason though. He was a funny, funny dude. A bad husband, but a funny dude.

Further, Kelly had immediately taken up with Bob. They were dating, and Bob had left his wife for Kelly, which we understood, because Bob's ex-wife Tina was fucking crazy and we only stayed friends with them for the kids.

We had always hoped Bob and Tina would break up, but that's because we assumed they would go away if they did. Molly had gone away as hoped, which was great, but Bob had not, which was not so great, and now we were stuck with him, as was Kelly.

The fact was, Bob hadn't been working for some time. We just didn't know it. He was like one of those unemployed Japanese guys who get dressed for work every day because they're too proud to tell anyone they've lost their job and then just sit in the park, suited up with nowhere to go.

Except Bob didn't even do that. Some days he sat in the Park Diner drinking coffee in his sweatpants, but most days he just sat in Thirsty's drinking one Yuengling after the next.

He had come clean to Kelly after he banged her and moved in; she was making a go of it, but it wasn't pretty, certainly not when he drank and raged about Obama and his inability to create jobs for honest, working Americans because Obama preferred to focus on Muslims and blacks and socialism and everything but the economy.

He wasn't raging tonight though, because tonight we were all here, and we were happy, drinking, talking, getting high and thinking about getting laid.

The kids were still running around as well, laughing, crying, jumping and screaming, full of joy and frolic.

You wouldn't have known that Kelly's son Josh had Asperger's, you couldn't tell tonight, and she hadn't mentioned immunizations even once, which was good, because one night after we had all been drinking for hours, she had said that her younger daughter Lucy would never be immunized like Josh had been and Bonnie had drunkenly called her a selfish parasite.

You also couldn't tell that Bonnie and Frank's daughter Sophie had cancer. She still had so much energy and spunk and vigor. She was beautiful and they coddled her, and if her illness maybe reminded Frank just a little too much of his brother dying when they were kids, he didn't let on much, not often anyway.

It's true that one night I had seen him crying on Lilly's shoulder, heaving actually, all the usual bluster gone, his handsome face swollen and ugly. I had maybe even seen them kiss before Lilly ran off, and it was okay, really, I figured it might even come in handy if I ever had a chance to get some alone time with Bonnie.

But that was for another night, a night when we weren't all so happy and full of glee, drinking and smoking, ignoring the rising flood waters, and hanging with friends, as our kids ran to and fro, darting about at our feet, all present, all in the moment, and all here.

A Different Story

"A PENNY FOR YOUR THOUGHTS," HE SAYS.

He is young, handsome, wearing a sharp gray suit, and crisp, white shirt.

I might have made love to him once based on his looks alone, but not now, I'm too old for that, for him. Not that I feel any different inside, it's just that the mirror behind the bar tells a different story. It tells me I am gray, and while I am still beautiful, I can't possibly be as beautiful as the person he's waiting for. She will be vibrant and dewy, melting into the seat next to him, oozing into his lap and claiming ownership.

I can't do that anymore. Still, I am here, and she is not, and so maybe this is my time, and my moment, as fleeting as it may be.

"I could tell you that I'm here because I don't want to be alone during the storm," I say, as the rain and wind start to build up outside the door which blows open with a boom and then slams shut every time someone walks in, "but I would like to seem more mysterious, when I'm sitting in a bar with a beautiful young man such as yourself."

"Okay, shoot," he says.

"Okay," I reply, "I'm thinking about how I don't dream anymore."

"I don't understand," he says, smiling this crooked smile.

"You can't," I say. "You are too young and full of hope. Even your disappointments are grand."

"Maybe," he says, "but I want to understand. I've done so little with my life, and I need to consume other people's experiences just to know what I want. I'm sort of like a vampire that way."

He adjusts his seat, and he is facing me.

I want to say something profound, though if not profound, sexy, both even, but I am momentarily struck dumb by how deep his dimples are, and whether I might be able to swim in them.

Unable to do that though, I instead take his face in my hands. His skin blanches, he is clearly taken aback, but he doesn't move, he just sits there, shaking ever so slightly. I'm amazed at what I've done, the heat rising in my cheeks. I don't move my hands though. Age has its benefits.

"What experiences of mine would you like to consume?" I ask, removing my hands from his face, and leaning back in my seat.

He grins.

"What did you dream about when you still dreamed?" he asks, more serious now.

"Wonderful things," I reply before taking a long drink from my gin and tonic. "Cold drinks and calloused hands, plunging naked into the river, its swollen waves buffeting me everywhere."

He is staring now, lost in something, awe maybe, confusion certainly, but it is mostly the idea that someone my age might be a sexual being.

Looking at him I am taken back to a party from so long ago. There was a boy just like this, young, eager, confident, and edible.

I told him I wanted a kiss for my birthday at midnight, and when he came to find me, we ate each other whole, and looking back now, it was as if destiny had alighted from the branches above us, to burn the memory of that moment, in that yard, into the far recesses of my brain, and ensure that a mere kiss, something ultimately so small in a larger life lived well, could have such a sense of immediacy so many years later.

"So why did you stop dreaming then?" he says leaning in again, practically panting.

I try to remember when the last time was that someone looked at me like that? But I don't know, or maybe I do, but I don't try to figure it out, instead I choose to linger for a moment in his gaze, soaking it up, holding on to it, not knowing when it may happen again.

"What was the point?" I reply.

"Dreaming is living," he says. "Without dreams we are merely robots, shells, not human."

"So, you're saying I'm not human?" I ask, grabbing his leg and leaning forward, my lips just centimeters from his.

"No-no-no," he stammers, pausing, staring, grabbing both of my legs with his hands, and sending an electric shock up my spine. "I just want you to feel something."

"I feel things," I respond, "paintings, and poetry, but you do get so alone, and you do forget how to feel, and then the dreams follow. Look, I'm going to freshen up, and when I come back, if you want to ride out the storm with an old woman, maybe you could help me feel something again."

"Okay," he says breathlessly, "I'll be right here."

I walk into the bathroom and I look at myself in the mirror. My face is flush, full of color, which only serves to highlight how gray my hair really is. Still, my lips remain full, my cheekbones high, this is real.

What does the young man see though?

Does he see what my long-time lover saw, fire and indiscretion?

What would this young man think if he knew that my lover would not leave his wife, could not, and that I knew he wouldn't, but I still waited for him to do so?

Would he think less of me? Would my strengths start to look like weaknesses?

And what would he think if he knew that my lover's wife banned me from the hospital when he was ill, but I was still able to get into his room as he lay there delusional and floating, and kiss him one last time as he drifted away from me, taking my dreams and anything that meant anything with him?

Would any of that mean anything to this young man, or does it only matter to me?

No matter, tonight is different, tonight there is promise. The storm has brought magic and kinetic energy, and one final taste of love, or something just like it.

I walk out of the bathroom, head held high, not too eager, but excited, twitchy, and proud.

The young man is kissing a young woman at the bar, his hands caught in her blonde hair, her leg jammed between his, both of them oblivious to the wider world.

I pause for a moment and linger as the windows rattle behind me, and then I walk out into the storm, the moment passed.

Longing

WE ARE SITTING BEHIND THEIR HOUSE. The chairs are plastic, Ikea I imagine, and the back deck while small, is nice, tree branches hanging overhead with year-round sparkly Christmas lights dancing between the leaves like little pulsating, multi-colored, stars.

The rain is coming hard and steady. They say it's the storm of the century. But we don't care, we are under the overhang, and we are here to drink.

It's what we, Lisa and I, do with them, Molly and Bruce. Someone comes into a bottle of something new, different, on a work trip, or vacation, maybe from some random visitor from out of town, and we drink it until it's gone, slowly for the most part, and civilized.

When the kids were younger we were more self-conscious about drinking until things got blurry or we couldn't walk home easily. Back then there were diapers to change and bottles to heat up.

Now we just let them run and run around Molly and Bruce's house, watching the same movies again and again, while we just drink and drink.

Tonight it's whiskey.

I could tell you that I don't have a problem with alcohol, but that's what problem drinkers tend to say, and I am not a problem drinker.

They also tend to say that I only drink when I want to, that I can stop whenever I want, and that it doesn't interfere with my life.

All of which I have definitely said, and all of which I mean.

Still, if you drink until things are blurry, and you cannot easily walk, and this despite the fact that your children are just steps away watching *Despicable Me* or chasing guinea pigs around the house, you might have a problem.

The real question I suppose is do I ever long for a drink, and the answer to that is yes, all the time. I can taste the alcohol hit my tongue even when it isn't there, and feel the warmth burn the back of my throat.

So, do I long for that, that feeling of being both alive and dead all at once? Yes, endlessly.

But it's all about longing, isn't it?

Or, more accurately, suppressing longing, the longing to be free, to wander, to be happy, and to be whatever I was supposed to before this happened—marriage, kids, Ikea chairs, and looking forward to backyard gatherings where I can forget all of it, who I am, and why this is the path I chose.

"Hey, faggot, wake up."

Huh?

Oh, I am the faggot, lost in my thoughts, and ignoring everyone.

"Where did you go Allen, and when the fuck are you coming back?"

It's Molly. She thinks she's funny, especially when she's drinking.

Lisa calls her a ball buster, but does so in a loving fashion. My mother would have called her earthy. No pretensions or false notes. No bullshit, blunt, yet rough.

Molly favors T-shirts where the sleeves stop at the shoulder, and skirts that stop just above the knees, the better to accentuate her biceps and calves.

Lisa loves Molly's muscles and how they ripple when Molly is talking.

Looking at her, it's amazing really how someone can mold themself into the version of themselves that they picture in their head. But that doesn't mean she doesn't look great, or that you can ever not turn your head when she walks by.

None of which is to say that Lisa doesn't look great too. She does. Not that I would ever say otherwise. And not that I am not happy she never asks me to compare her appearance to that of Molly's. Not that she would though, that would be crazy.

Bruce on the other hand, not much muscle there. No ripple. He's all upstate Irish, doughy and pale. Pink even, like a manatee. But with these beautiful soft-looking hands, and this curiosity about everything that is so appealing. Things like Sabermatrics or cooking with liquid nitrogen, things I don't normally care about, but that he makes seem interesting, leaving me hanging on every word.

He's like a poet. Not that Molly cares. Which is okay too, because Bruce doesn't care that she doesn't care, and she doesn't care that he doesn't care, it's like an agreement, and it works for them.

Still, I always feel like Molly's missing something, something amazing, and you know how it is, with kids and work and bills, sometimes marriage is more like a partnership. But that passes eventually, right? I hope so.

There is a crack of lightning overhead and the skies briefly light up. I close my eyes for a moment to take it in, such a wonderful sound, like bowling balls smashing into pins.

It's funny though, as I try to take in the night, the smell of the rain, the crashing skies, I think about Bruce again, his hands, how soft looking they are, and for a moment I am longing for them to touch me, and I wonder just how strong the whiskey is.

Suddenly a jolt goes up my bare leg, just below the end of my khaki shorts. A hand is there, just sitting there briefly.

Lisa.

So lovely she is, and yes, marriage may be a trap, but that isn't because of her, I know that, she loves me, we work.

"Dude, how's that whiskey, huh?"

I open my eyes and its Bruce touching my leg, not Lisa.

Fuck.

I look at him and I think to myself, is this maybe what longing is? Wanting something enough to make it true? Maybe, and yet, what if you don't really know you want something until it is right there in front of you? What do you call that?

"Uh, yeah, it's great," I say.

"I picked it up in Tennessee when I was traveling there for work last week," Bruce says. "I met a guy who knew a guy and here we are."

"Yeah," I say, "here we are."

But where am I really and why hasn't Bruce moved his hand? I go to brush it away, but it's gone already. It was the feeling that lingered, not him.

I am reminded of the time in high school, when the kid who lived down the street touched my leg at his pool. It was just the two of us, it was dusk, and we were lounging around, drinking beers, trying to soak up the last of the sun. He was so beautiful, and I had been thinking about him all the time then, looking for chances to see him, talk to him, lounge with him.

On that day, with the light setting, his hair all long, he looked like a god, and when he touched my leg trying to get my attention, I came, suddenly and explosively. Nothing like that had ever happened before, and nothing like that has happened since, not after he ran into his house certainly, and not after he avoided eye contact with me until I stopped trying to get his attention, much less anyone else's.

And now here is Bruce, and we are in his backyard, our wives just feet away, and I realize just how often I look for him in the neighborhood, or at pick-up after school. Hoping to run into him, hoping to say hello, maybe get his undivided attention for just a little while. I realize that the feeling of longing has returned, though maybe it never really went away.

I jump up and shake my head, trying to clear it, trying to chase away the thoughts that still linger like his touch did just moments ago.

"What is it?" Lisa asks.

She looks concerned, but is it for me, or her? How many lies can I live, and how much longing can I deny and expect her not to know something?

"We're going to go," Lisa says, "it's late."

"Okay mama," Molly says before kissing her on the lips and lingering for just a moment beyond appropriate.

"You bitch," Lisa says pulling away, at first laughing, then crying.

"What?" Molly says. "What did I do?"

"It's nothing," I say, "it's nothing you did. It's the drink, and the storm, and it's late, that's all."

"All right," Bruce says, grabbing my shoulders. "We'll do this again soon, yes?"

I look at Bruce, hoping to see something in his eyes, something that says that I am not crazy, and that I am not alone in feeling what I feel. But I can't tell if anything is there at all. Maybe I will ask him some time though, maybe.

I gather the kids and we wobble home, dodging the downed trees and scattered garbage cans.

As I climb into bed next to Lisa who is looking away from me and feigning sleep, I realize that I am never going to say a word to Bruce, not a chance, and I resolve instead to just start drinking less.

Night Swimming

I OPEN THE WINDOW on the back porch and begin pushing and prying the plywood off that covers it. At first there is no give, but soon there is movement, cracking, and a web-like splinter racing along the board as it bends, then shatters in my bare hands.

I'm hit with a blast of muddy air as a tree branch immediately pushes its way through the window, followed by the fecund, swampy smell of the storm as it blows through the backyard, tossing the smaller trees and bushes to and fro.

When the board is in pieces at my feet, I remove my shirt, wrap it around my hand, and punch through the remaining glass which is hanging before me like jagged teeth.

I carefully step through the window, my jeans and Air Jordans still on, little rivulets of blood now streaking down my back. I lower myself into the flood waters that are crashing their way down South Mountain and cascading through the neighborhood.

I hold onto the window frame for one moment, then two, and

then take a deep breath before letting go and swimming into the maul of water now surrounding me.

This had not been the plan.

The actual plan had been simple. The storm would come and I would embrace the rat-tat-tat of the rain hitting my house as I sat alone on the back porch.

I would use the time to think, to reflect on a life lost not only to poor decisions, but worse than that, no decisions.

I would certainly dwell on the women I could have fucked, the mistakes I made, the times I was too scared to pull the trigger, to commit myself to living, if not an actual life, at least living in the moment right there before me.

I would also think about the endless roads not taken, especially the places I might have lived—New Orleans, Santa Cruz, Bangkok—and the adventures I might have embarked on, hiking to Machu Pichu or wandering through Alaska, if I just could have somehow willed myself to take one step, followed by another.

Inevitably, I would have thought about the loss of both my mother and father to cancer, the cells in their body turning on them, twisting into the enemy, and how I sat with them in the cancer ward at Two Rivers General, with the endless drip, drip, drip of the chemo, the old people and their yellow skin, and me always wondering if how they had lived, with regret and anger, played some role in their demise.

I would have certainly contemplated how, and when, my brother and I stopped talking, because this to me is the greatest tragedy in a not semi-tragic life, that could have been better, or at least different, and more complete, even if I never made sense of these other things.

Was it a girl that came between us? It must have been, what else is there, though maybe it was money, because if it isn't women, it's money, who gets what, and how much of it, and on and on.

But I just don't know anymore.

Anyway, that had been the plan, but then there was the rain, and the memories, the regret, the might-have-beens, and I decide that what I'm really going to do is what I'm best at, get fucked up, and forget the day, the month, and everything that came before it.

So I laid out my supplies: ten pepperoni Slim Jims, a bag of cheddar cheese Combos, one bottle of Maker's Mark, a twelve-pack of Yuengling, half a dozen tightly rolled joints, and a bag of mushrooms.

I also had my laptop and the porn I downloaded to get me through the storm. I favor blondes, but mainly it has to be amateur, home-made, lo-fi, and desperate, normal people trying to look good and get off while a camera is probing their otherwise most private moments.

My wife Jessica never liked porn, or booze, much less staying put anywhere, and she would not have enjoyed riding out the storm of the century like this.

But she has been gone how long now? I couldn't say.

One night I went out on the porch to smoke a joint and listen to the Ramones, a nice high and two minutes of thrash, just enough to calm my nerves, and then I had drifted off. When I awoke to the sun poking through the window, she was gone, no note, no nothing.

There's no sun poking through the window now though, but it is rattling, as the tree branches outside bend and scrape across the plywood covering it.

I am hunkered down on the couch and I light a joint. As the burn hits my throat I think about all of the loss piling upon itself like a nest, my wife, my parents, my brother, and it's all too much.

I take another drag and the smoke wraps itself around my brain in a hazy, beautiful hug. I plan to start the Maker's Mark next, but I start coughing, first small hacks, more like hiccups, and then bigger ones, wracking my head and soon my whole body, leaving me convulsing on the couch.

When the coughing finally subsides, there is nothing I want more than fresh air. After that I start tearing off the plywood that covers the back window.

My temptation with the flood waters coursing over and around me is to fight it somehow, seeking to control something that cannot be controlled by man, but that's not going to work, I have no control, and I can either choose to go with the flow or perish in my backyard.

I push myself towards the current, and start to do the crawl, stroke, stroke, lift head, breathe, stroke, stroke, lift head, breathe, and though there are branches and garbage can lids all around me, I soon have a groove, and I am swimming, graceful as a dolphin, and passing from my yard into the next, and then on and on after that.

I zip by Billy Knox's house, the doctor who said my father was too sick for the trial that may have saved his life. For a moment I contemplate swimming to his back door, tearing the boards from it, and punching him in the face in front of his wife Frankie and their terrified kids. But I'm already so tired, and all of that seems so long ago, a moment refracted through a memory that has slowly lost its power to enrage me, buried there like a bruise, and only painful when exposed.

A wave of water crashes over me as I reach the end of my block and turn onto the main street into town. The current is stronger here, as water pours in from the backyards on both sides of the block. There are more branches here too, though more space as well, and I soon see that if I shift from the crawl to the breast stroke, I can easily steer between them.

I also find that I am terribly short of breath, and that even pausing for a moment to coast with the tide is an effort. I wonder now if I've made a mistake, and roll onto my back and try to float for awhile.

As I float, I watch the big rain drops continue to fall from the sky, splattering my chest and face, and remember yet again the drip, drip, drip of the cancer ward, the stark white walls, the quiet, how old everyone looks with their gray, ashy skin and wispy strands of hair.

I'm not thinking back to my mother or father though, or ruminating on the malformed cells that strangled their final days. I'm looking forward and thinking about my own doctor's appointment just days ago, when it was still quiet, no rain, or broken branches, and no night swimming.

"You have lung cancer," the doctor said. "We'll do what we can, but if I can be frank, I would get your house in order."

I take one last look at the endless sky, close my eyes and concentrate on embracing the massive rain drops melting into my face. I then flip back onto my stomach, start to swim again, turn onto a side street, and call on my last bit of energy to forge into the tide, and up the hill before me.

When I'm not sure I can tack on even one more stroke, I realize I've made it to my destination, and I drag myself onto my brother's porch.

I lay there for a moment, thinking about what I might say, but no words come to me. I stand up, and as I find myself doubled-over, my cough returning, head swimming, I knock on his door.

Something Like This

IT WAS AN AGREEMENT, tacit and understood.

It's what people do over time when they are in love. They ask things of one another. They have expectations. Sometimes spoken, other times stated less overtly, the request based more in how they react, or don't react, to the things happening around them.

We were watching a movie one night. We were on the couch. There was popcorn, Twizzlers, a comforter that had flowers all over it, and little twisty vines.

The dogs were lying at our feet, sleeping, their backs rising with each breath, and it was dark, except for the glow of the television which was lighting up Jen's beautiful face and illuminating her hair like a halo.

Did she look like an angel? Maybe, I thought so, but I was in love. I am in love. Despite what's happened, where we are now, and what she has become.

Love dies for many reasons, or worse, fades, but it doesn't stop because of something like this, a disease, or virus, or whatever. It changes, and you adapt, molding it to fit this new way of being. You have to, otherwise you have to let it go, and who wants to do that?

I remember the first time I saw her. We were at Thirsty's. I was walking over to the pool table, and she was standing there talking to some friends. Our eyes met just as she ran her fingers through her hair, smiling and turning towards me.

I couldn't look away, and I didn't want to, I was locked in, for good, for life.

I don't know if it's healthy to be with just one person, to be exclusive and monogamous, and I don't care what others think about their own marriages, how they treat them, if they stray or make arrangements. It's all fine with me, marriage doesn't have to be something sacred, or one size fits all.

I'm just talking about myself, her, us, that was it. I was done, everything before was dead to me, other relationships, other women, all of it. I was happy, content, it's embarrassing, I know that, but it was what it was, and I didn't question it, I didn't have to, it was good, we were good.

And so we are on the couch that night. There is the glow, the smell of popcorn, the dogs, our legs all akimbo under the blanket. Julia Stiles was on the screen. Or maybe it was Piper Perabo? It doesn't matter. It was someone young and pretty, interchangeable, and she was in a car, or on a boat, maybe a bus. There was a crash, or an explosion, something loud and potentially life-altering, and suddenly she was laying on a street, or a dock, and there was an ambulance, and Channing Tatum, or maybe Zac Effron, was running in the rain, possibly in a military uniform, or doctor's scrubs, something, but they were running, through the city streets, or maybe along a country road, not that it matters, because the point is, they had to be there, with her, loving her, and trying to make everything all right through the sheer force of that love.

But they couldn't make it all right. All they could do is get there at that last moment, the rain, sweat, and tears glistening on their cheeks. Or possibly, maybe, even their bare torso. But glistening surely, and as she was lying there on the street, or on a stretcher, or maybe even in the hospital already, he cradled her head in his soft, manly hands and he said, "I love you, now and forever, and only you, no matter what," and she looked at him, and with her last bit of strength she stroked his handsome, stubbled cheek, and she said, "I love you too, in this world and the next, but when it's time, and it's going to be time soon, you need to let me go, please, no extraordinary measures, I don't want to live like this, I can't." "Of course, anything," he replied, even though he was dying inside, broken and destroyed, as everything he had known was spinning out of control and slowly slipping away.

At this point, Jen looked up, her eyes speaking to me like that day at Thirsty's, and I knew right there, she was saying, no extraordinary measures for me either. Don't let me live like that, I can't, please, and if you have to kill me to make it so, do it, smother me, cut my air tube, whatever, however, just do it, promise me.

I squeezed her hand, and I let her know that I understood, and that yes, I would kill her if it came to that, I loved her too much not to.

And I meant it, I did, but this, this is different, right, this virus, or whatever it is?

There was the rain that wouldn't stop, the storm of the century they said, and then the darkness and chaos that descended upon us so suddenly, stealing our lives, our sense of right and wrong, making us question what we thought we knew, the rules and norms and all the things we had lived by, all of it gone, leaving us a world we didn't know anymore, or understand, a world no longer of the living.

No one planned for this, and I so I have to wonder, in this new world, the world after the flood, do my obligations to her remain the same? Because while Jen is still here, it is only as a memory, no thoughts, or empathy, just a rotting shell, and there is nothing extraordinary about that. It's who she is now, but am I obligated to kill what she's become? Because this is different isn't it?

She wouldn't think so, but do I really know that? No, I don't know, I don't know anything anymore, and I don't care, and so instead she is in our basement, shuffling around, guttural, craving flesh and blood, and I have been feeding her, I have to.

At first it was our dogs, and then the feral cats wandering the neighborhood, their homes washed away, their owners having taken flight, or worse, forced to wander Two Rivers themselves, directionless and hungry, and now I've been forced to feed her whatever else still remains, errant squirrels, and the occasional bloated bodies that suddenly emerge from the mucky waters with their still beating hearts.

How long can this go on though?

I don't know that either, but there is another option. Instead of killing her, I could join her. I could let her consume me, and we could become one, always, and forever.

That was the plan anyway, wasn't it?

She is just steps away, and then an embrace, and what would be so bad about that?

Consider the alternative, being alone, both of us dead in our own ways, and what's that, that's nothing.

Nothing I ever wanted certainly.

Things Start

HOW DID IT START?

With a bump and a thud, or maybe it's a thud followed by a bump, not that the bump thud order of things is truly important.

How it started though, that is important. It's everything.

One minute there isn't a body stuck to the front grill of your car and the next minute there is. Not that you notice this until you and your wife get home, leave your car, find blood splattered across the hood and see the twisted body hanging there and not moving.

So, it sort of starts like that. Though even that arguably isn't how it starts.

Maybe it starts when you first meet in college, so taken with her legs and ass that your heart skips a beat, your brain briefly enters a fugue state, and you find yourself wandering around campus wondering how and where you will run into her ass again.

Or, maybe it's the first time you wake up next to her in bed, her naked body luminescent in the morning light. She is so still and her breaths are so minimal it's like looking at a perfectly preserved corpse, something oddly erotic and discomfiting all at once.

Or, or, what about when she gave birth to your son, maybe it started then, splayed out as she was, legs everywhere, fluids flying, first his head, and then his slippery, muck-covered body somehow emerging from the improbably small space before you, a moment so peculiarly menacing and surreal it's more like magic than science.

It could have been any of that, or all of it, they are moments when some things start, and other things become something else, some of which are momentous, though ultimately having little to do with this, this thing that didn't really start in any of those places, but is still somehow connected, because everything is connected, and that's just how it works.

You are in the car with your wife, it is the storm of the century, and you are not thinking about her ass, well you probably are, still, always, but at that moment generally speaking you are not thinking about her ass, falling in love, or the miracle that is birth.

No, you've just had a fight, which is something people can do when not caught up in the miracles and moments of glorious oneness that is their life together.

So, how did that start?

Well, that was stupid. You weren't being honest. Your wife received a text, the phone glowing and beeping and taking her away from where you had been, a conversation about your kids' school, Thanksgiving, your new data plan, mostly stuff about nothing, or everything, it was what married people talk about, endlessly, the regular stuff that allows you to get to the other stuff, the more important things that can sometimes be hard to address.

But then the text came in and she smiled.

That's all really, just a smile, but you knew it was that dude from the office, the guy she always calls her work husband, the young, single one, who has some weird sexual fluidity thing going on that allows him to sleep with men or women depending on his mood, something you find confusing and your wife finds fascinating.

You don't think she's fucking him, but she's doing something, something she says you don't understand, because you cannot accept that men and women can just be friends, and that she needs to have a male friend she can confide in who doesn't look at her as an object to be undressed and conquered, just a woman in all her nonsexual womanness.

And how can you argue with that? You can't.

Plus, you know you are not a great listener, and maybe neither of you have been doing very much listening to the other one for some time now, something you just didn't recognize while you were in the middle of all that other stuff.

You could possibly say something about that listening thing right now as she sits there smiling and staring at her phone, because in this moment all that not talking you've not been doing seems so much more obvious to you and you wonder if it does to her as well. Actually addressing it though, here, now, finding the right words, that seems so hard, which you know is a backwards way to think about it, but you also know that's it not going to happen, it can't, won't, and so instead you say, please don't text while I'm driving in the rain, it's distracting.

She doesn't listen to you though. She doesn't seem to hear you at all, so you reach for her cell phone and she turns away.

Now, should you be doing that while you are driving? You should not. Are you thinking about this? No, you aren't doing much thinking at all apparently.

Should you pause here then, maybe catch your breath, remember that you are in the car and it's raining, that you've been a really poor listener, that you still really love her ass despite what may or may not be going on with the dude, and that there has to be a better way?

Yes, you should pause, but you don't, which is another way things start, not pausing, but it's too late, you are enraged and you lunge for her phone, still driving, not looking, just lunging, and there is a bump and a thud, or a thud followed by a bump, and that's how it starts, with a lunge, and a cell phone, a text, the storm of the century, and some fucking sexually fluid guy from work.

Neither of you acknowledge the thud, however, or the bump, much less the text, the rain, or any of it for the rest of the drive home. Neither of you even says a word. What can you say?

When you get home though you both silently walk to the front of the car to see if there is any damage, and there it is, a body, an actual body, stuck there, twisted, and molded to the grill.

And you should definitely say something about this, right, yes, but what, what can someone say about this when they can't even talk about all of the things they should actually be talking about?
Not much. Not much at all.

So instead, you go get your shovel, and that's how it really starts.

Acknowledgements

So many thanks, and bound to miss many at that, but for what it's worth, thanks to Jason Pettus and CCLaP, all of the journals that saw it fit to print these pieces in one form or another, my hometown of Binghamton, NY, Richard Linklater, Junot Diaz and Elizabeth Crane Brandt, and her fellow blurbers, Sara Lippmann, Leesa Cross-Smith, Tim Horvath, Dave Newman, Michael Czyzniejewski, Debbie, the boys, my mom Judy, brother Adam, and his crew, Thirsty's and the Park Diner, and as always, Rod Serling and *The Twilight Zone*.

BEN TANZER is the author of the books *99 Problems, My Father's House, You Can Make Him Like You, Orphans,* which won the 24th Annual Midwest Book Award in Fantasy/SciFi/Horror/Paranormal and a Bronze medal in the Science Fiction category at the 2015 IPPY Awards, and *Lost in Space,* which received an Honorable Mention in the Chicago Writers Association 2014 Book Awards Traditional Non-Fiction category, among others. He has also contributed to *Punk Planet, Clamor,* and *Men's Health,* serves as Senior Director, Acquisitions for Curbside Splendor, and can be found online at *This Blog Will Change Your Life.*

49727892R00135

Made in the USA
Lexington, KY
18 February 2016